Hasmonean Primary
School

This book has been donated by

Talia Keryn +
Gideon Miller
Audrey Davar

A FACE
at the
WINDOW

Meir Uri Gottesman

CIS
P·U·B·L·I·S·H·E·R·S
New York · London · Jerusalem

Copyright © 1989

First Printing: 1989
Second Printing: 2000

Published & Distributed by:
C.I.S. Publishers & Distributors
180 Park Avenue
Lakewod, New Jersey 08701
(732) 905-3000   Fax: (732) 367-6666

Book and Cover Design: Ronda Kruger Israel
Cover Illustration: Gregg Hinlicky
Typography: Chaya Hoberman

ISBN 1-56062-017-X Hardcover
       1-56062-018-8 Softcover

PRINTED IN THE UNITED STATES OF AMERICA

Dedicated to my beloved children עמו״ש

Aron Aryeh, Elisheva Rivka, Avraham Yosef
Yoska, Yitzchak Isaac, Pesach Nachman
Baruch Simcha, Shulamith Tova
Nechama Dina, Yisrael Mordechai.

Table of Contents

1 ✍ The Strange Neighbor 9
2 ✍ Luzer the Shmoozer 16
3 ✍ A Surprise Meeting 24
4 ✍ Shabbos Shirah 30
5 ✍ Super Student 40
6 ✍ The Missing Piece 49
7 ✍ A Special Gift 55
8 ✍ A Secret Rendezvous 65
9 ✍ A Moment of Shock 70
10 ✍ Nightmare City 80
11 ✍ A Difficult Decision 84
12 ✍ Izzy and Dizzy 92
13 ✍ An Act of Revenge 97
14 ✍ The Invisible Court 102
15 ✍ Kiddush Levana 108
16 ✍ The Hidden Ravine 113
17 ✍ The Trunk in the Basement 121
18 ✍ The Atom Bomb Satchel 132

1   The Strange Neighbor

THE SKY GREW DARKER AND DARKER, AND THE WINDS BLEW cold. Rabbi Mordechai Levi sat in his place in the *shul*, trying to concentrate on the small Hebrew letters in front of him. From time to time, he lifted his head from the old *Chumash* and counted heads. Miriam, his eleven year old daughter, watched as her father checked the clock and then the door. Soon, it would be way past sunset and too late for the Friday afternoon *Minchah* service. There were only nine men in their little basement synagogue, and ten were needed for a *minyan*. No tenth man, no *minyan*.

The door swung open, and everyone in the *shul* looked

up expectantly. No one came in, and the door clattered.

"It's just the wind," grumbled old Mr. Goldberg as he fiddled with his glasses.

"Someone close the door. It's freezing down here," ordered Mr. Eisenberg, who always complained, hot or cold.

Rabbi Levi, who had stood up with hope, sighed and sagged back into his place. Israel and Daniel, Miriam's ten and eight year old brothers, moved to stand near their father like protecting soldiers. Instinctively, they knew it made him feel better to have them close. Though their real names were Israel and Daniel, everyone called Israel "Izzy" and Daniel "Dizzy."

Miriam loved watching her father. He sat over his *shtender*, his snowy white beard cascading over the old *Chumash*, a large glistening black velvet *yarmulka* crowning his head, his long silken black gabardine coat flowing down to his ankles. Behind him, row atop row, were the large volumes of the Talmud, old brown covers stamped in fading gold letters, mystic books of the *Kabbalah*, *Chassidic* works and sets of the *Shulchan Aruch*. Their little *shul* had everything!

Everything except a *minyan*.

The children knew what was coming next, and they dreaded it. Their father looked up from his *sefer*, summoned Miriam and turned to all three.

"Children, we need a *minyan*," he said. "No one else is coming. Schwartz and Greenstein are away. Kornblau is sick. Please go out and find someone."

"But, Tati!" protested Dizzy. "It's cold out there."

Rabbi Levi didn't answer. He just lifted his huge eyebrows. That was enough. High eyebrows meant no arguing.

The children looked at each other, shrugged and threw on their coats.

Rabbi Levi's little *shul* was in the basement of his home, a few houses east of Bathurst Street. That was his problem. He had never registered his *shul* officially, so he could not put up a sign announcing it. If he did, neighbors might complain, and his *minyan* would disappear.

"Why do we always have to do this?" grumbled Izzy. His glasses were getting frosted over in the cold and slipping down his skinny nose like ice cubes.

"I'm going back home. It's freezing out here," chimed in Dizzy. The wind lifted his *yarmulka* off his head, and he had forgotten his scarf.

"Quiet, you two. No one is going anywhere," Miriam warned. "Tati needs a *minyan*. Do you want Tati's Shabbos ruined?"

That quieted them. They all loved their father and wouldn't want him sad if they could help it. But in her heart Miriam wished that a *minyan* could be nine men, just once.

They stood on the corner of Bathurst and Sandringham, waiting and watching. It was late, and the street lights had gone on. Izzy held on to a street pole and leaned out like a sailor before the mast, to see if he could spot someone.

A man was coming! They saw him a block away, huddled against the wind, trying to hold onto his hat. They waited for him to walk the block and cross the street, and then they sprung out. Miriam blocked his way, and the boys boxed him in from either side.

"Please," pleaded Miriam. "We have nine men. Could you help us make a *minyan*?"

The man huddled tighter, impatient.

"How can I come to you if they're waiting for me in the

Old Shul? I've been *davening* there for fifteen years."

"But they have a *minyan* there without you," argued Izzy boldly.

The man just hunkered himself tighter against the cold, grunted and walked past them.

"He didn't have to be so sour about it," grumbled Miriam under her breath.

They continued waiting, their faces growing used to the cold and stinging wind. But they had one unstoppable enemy, hidden behind ashen clouds. Yehoshua had stopped the sun once, but they couldn't. The time for *Minchah* was slipping away.

"No one is coming out in this cold," whined Dizzy. "Why do we have to wait?"

Miriam sighed. Big-mouthed Dizzy was right. Everyone who went to *shul* was there already. She was angry.

"Tati will be heartbroken, but you're right. It's just not fair."

She blew a strand of her dark red hair straight up in frustration, and snowflakes melted down her face.

They turned back towards the house. Two houses down, Miriam stopped and eyed a doorway. Izzy and Dizzy watched her with growing dismay. She looked at them, and they looked at her.

"No, Miriam, please," begged Izzy.

"No way, Miri, no way. Forget it, Bubie," pleaded Dizzy.

"But Tati needs a *minyan*," argued Miriam. "He hasn't missed a *minyan* since he started the *shul*. It'll break his heart."

Dizzy was not impressed.

"You are not knocking at that house, Miriam."

"Miri, please," echoed Izzy.

Miriam saw that Izzy was weakening. She did not like the idea of knocking on that door either. A weird family lived there, the Kranzes, father and daughter. There seemed to be no mother. They were almost never seen, by day or by night. Occasionally, Miriam saw the girl come home from school. She never smiled, never looked right or left, never played outside.

Weird. But they were Jewish. A neighbor had mentioned that to her mother. And a Jewish man, even a weird Jewish man, makes a *minyan*. Miriam's love for her father overcame her fear. She blew away a snow-soaked curl from her face, which showed she meant business.

"If you boys walk me to the Kranz door, you can get a big bag of chips after *Shabbos*."

"No way," said Dizzy, looking at Izzy for support.

"Two bags then, one for each of you. Any flavor."

"Could I get barbecue?" asked Izzy, softening.

"Barbecue, corn . . ."

"Ridges?" pressed Dizzy.

"Ridges. But we have to go right now."

"You promise?" demanded Dizzy. Miriam's word was not always that reliable.

"I promise. But come on!"

Hesitantly, Izzy and Dizzy followed Miriam up the three short steps leading to the entrance. There was a light coming from inside, so someone was home.

Miriam knocked, softly. They waited. No answer. The wind howled stronger, blowing her scarf in her face. It was so cold. Miriam knocked again, a bit harder. They had knocked on other doors before and knew what sounds to listen for. The slightest rustle, muffled footsteps, a door swinging open, all indicated that someone was home, someone was coming. Izzy put his ear against the door, lifted it and shook his head. No sound.

"I'll do it," insisted Dizzy. He ran up to the door, and banged hard with all his might. Too hard. The force of his banging knocked the door open by itself.

The children stood frozen, agape at what they saw.

The hallway opened to a living room that led to the back dining room, just as in their own home. In their home, bright lights were on everywhere. Here, everything was dim and dark. The Kranz girl sat on a chair, underneath a chandelier with just one bulb in it. Her head was bowed in sadness. Over her stood her father, seething with fury.

Miriam, Izzy and Dizzy stood frozen. The man, too, was stunned to see them, and stood staring. The girl's eyes opened wide, focusing on Miriam. It was like a film frozen in mid-frame.

"What are you doing here?" shouted the man.

The film was running again. He strode towards the children, his thin face set with rage. Izzy and Dizzy turned and bolted out the door, leaving Miriam to face his charge.

"We . . . we . . . I was looking for a *minyan* for our *shul*." Miriam was so frightened she could hardly speak.

"What are you doing in my house?" bellowed the man. "Who gave you permission to come in here?"

He arched over her now, crowding her between himself and the half-closed door. Miriam expected to be struck. She could not stop herself from crying.

"Nothing," she sobbed, angry at herself that she was so babyish. "My brother knocked too hard on the door and it swung open by itself. We were just trying to get a tenth man for our *minyan*. The door just opened. I'm sorry."

"You're a liar," shouted the man. "You were trying to rob

me! You and those little thieves."

Miriam shook her head. She wanted to argue, but the words stuck in her throat. She looked up at the little girl seated at the table, and their eyes locked for a moment.

The man turned to follow Miriam's gaze. His hard, pale face grew even more contorted.

"What are you staring at? What business do you have with her? What business do you have here, thief! Get out of my house. Get out of my house!"

Miriam nodded, not able to speak. All she wanted in the world was to get out of this house, to get away from this horrible, crazy man.

"Get out!" he hissed, his face menacingly close to hers.

Miriam turned to leave, but something made her look back to the pathetic girl sitting at the table. Their eyes brushed for a second.

She's trying to talk to me, Miriam thought. She's talking to me with her eyes.

She turned and ran out into the cold, pure air, her tears mingling with the snow flakes. She was furious at her brothers who had left her to face that man. If she got her hands on Izzy and Dizzy, they would be sorry!

2 Luzer the Shmoozer

THE LEVI HOME WAS AS WARM AND BRIGHT AND COLORFUL inside as it was bleak and cold outside. Miriam ran up the front steps, slipped off her boots and ran into the large living-dining room. The chandelier blazed over the dining room table, where her mother was reading a newspaper column on the weekly Torah portion. From downstairs came the boisterous sound of men singing.

"We have a *minyan?*" asked Miriam, astonished.

Leah Levi looked up.

"Yes," she said. "At the last minute. Luzer the Shmoozer turned up." She removed her reading glasses and studied

Miriam's face. "Miriam, what's the matter?"

Miriam had not thought to wash her face, and it was a mess of dribbling hair, melted snow and tear stains. Now I'm in for it, she thought. A million questions. Then her father would hear what happened with that Mr. Kranz, throw on his coat and run out in the cold. And his health couldn't take it.

Miriam wasn't going to tell a lie. But she didn't have to tell all the truth.

"We knocked at the Kranz door."

Leah Levi's brows knitted, then her deep blue eyes suddenly grew large.

"Kranz? You mean two houses down? What business did you have going there? He's such a strange person."

"But Tati needed a *minyan*." Miriam was growing upset again, but she vowed she would not cry. She bit her lip.

"I don't care. We don't need it so badly that you had to go over there. They're . . ." Leah Levi struggled to find a polite word. ". . . very different."

Very different, all right, thought Miriam. It's very, very different to stand over your helpless child and scare the daylights out of her.

"So, what happened?" Miriam's mother persisted.

"He refused."

"No? He just said no? Is that why you were crying?"

Miriam thought fast. She just wanted to forget about Mr. Kranz. She didn't want anything to do with him. She was afraid. She just wanted to forget it.

"Well, he was rude. Very rude. I wasn't really crying that much. It's snow on my face."

Leah Levi gave Miriam a long look, a look that said, "Come on, tell me the truth, the whole story." But Miriam stood calmly, quietly enduring the Mommy X-Ray.

"Go upstairs and wash your face," Leah finally said. "David the folk singer is coming to the *seudah*, as well as Luzer."

Miriam groaned.

"Oh no, not Luzer."

"Go. Hurry."

Miriam went up to wash her face. Through the heating ducts, the voices of the men filtered up to her room and ran through all the walls of the house. It was as if the house itself was singing *Lecha Dodi*.

Shabbos felt different in the Levi household. Someone had turned on the lights *in* everyone. Everything shone.

In the dining room, an extra long table covered with a glistening white tablecloth stretched across the room. In the center of the table was a crystal vase with flowers, and a five stemmed silver candelabra, where five candles flickered like little jewels.

Miriam had stood at her mother's side when she recited the *berachah* over the candles, and prayed for the family's good health. As she prayed, the wispy smoke of the candles rose upward, as though they carried up the message.

The table was set simply but neatly. There were always extra settings for guests. In the front of the table was a crystal decanter of sweet red wine, a large silver goblet and two giant *challos* covered with a white velvet cloth embroidered with the words *Shabbos Kodesh* in gold letters.

Leah and Miriam waited to see what guests Rabbi Levi would fish up from the *minyan*. There was always someone at the Levi table, from Toronto, from Israel, from South America, from every corner of the globe where Jews lived.

Meshulachim, visiting rabbis who came to raise money for hospitals, for *yeshivos* or poor families, always found a place at the Levi table. Some were polite. Some had poor manners. Some had short, grizzled beards, others had long flowing beards like Miriam's father.

All were interesting. They told the inside news of what was really happening in this city or that, shared insights on *Chumash* or Talmud, complimented the food, asked the children questions, sang far-off melodies, ate heartily and made every Friday night a party. They also kept Izzy and Dizzy under control. The boys didn't dare argue or grab each other's silverware when guests sat next to them.

But Rabbi Levi did not limit his guests to religious Jews. He was always looking for new "business," strangers to draw under his wing and introduce to Yiddishkeit. You never knew whom he would invite for dinner. You could never tell whom he would meet in the street, or on a bus, or at the hospital. That's how he met David the folk singer, while waiting for a bus on Bathurst Street. Rabbi Levi had a beard, David had a beard; so naturally he insisted that David join them for a Sabbath meal.

There was the sound of scuffling and muffled arguing on the steps. That meant *davening* was over and Izzy and Dizzy were fighting their way up. There was the sound of "Good Shabbos," and then Rabbi Levi appeared at the door of the dining room, beaming with *Shabbos* joy. Tagging behind him shyly was David, trying to stay in the background.

And then came Luzer the Shmoozer.

Miriam groaned to herself. Not Luzer. Not again. The family always referred to him as Luzer the Shmoozer, Luzer the Talker. He always had something to say about everything.

Luzer was big, very big, like a tall sack of potatoes that bulged in the middle. He had three, maybe four, chins. He wore an oversize brownish orange hat, a wide green tie, a tan jacket and checkered gray pants. Everything was faded and stained, and looked forty years old. And Luzer never changed his outfit. Never.

Whenever Luzer came to a Friday night service, Rabbi Levi invited him up for the meal. It was a *mitzvah*, the rabbi repeatedly reminded his family, and not all *mitzvos* are easy. The trouble was that Luzer was a human vacuum cleaner. He ate the family off the table.

Rabbi Levi stood at the head of the table, with the chandelier glistening over his head, and summoned Miriam, Izzy and Dizzy to stand around him. He was flanked by his wife Leah on one side, with David and Luzer on the other. He lifted his pale white hands over the childrens' heads and intoned the Friday night *berachah*.

He kissed Miriam and the boys on the forehead. It was the favorite moment of the whole week for Miriam. She felt very close to her parents.

Together, the family and guests sang *Shalom Aleichem*. Three times over they chanted the lovely melody. Even Izzy and Dizzy calmed down and acted almost human. Except for Luzer. He was already surveying the table, the salads, the olives and pickles, checking out his silverware and fingering his wine glass.

Miriam's father lifted the cup, looked to all those gathered around the table and recited *Kiddush*. He had hardly sat down to sip from his cup of wine when Luzer had his cup out, impatiently beckoning for his sip of wine. Miriam and her mother looked at each other, Dizzy rolled his eyes skyward, and David made believe he didn't see what was happening. Rabbi Levi had hardly finished filling all the cups when Luzer was back, his cup outstretched again.

Carefully, he poured Luzer more wine.

Rabbi Levi rose, and the family marched into the kitchen to wash their hands. A blessed silence fell on the room, but there were lots of hand gestures, grunts and fiddling with silverware as they waited for Rabbi Levi to return. He whipped off the white and gold *challah* cover, revealing two huge, golden *challos* with raisins in them. Luzer drooled.

Rabbi Levi lifted both loaves in his large hands, fingers caressing each of them like a precious baby, recited the *berachah* and distributed the pieces to everyone.

The meal began.

Luzer went to work. For Luzer, eating without *challah* was not eating. He used *challah* for everything. *Challah* was his spoon and his fork, and sometimes his napkin. It took three slices for Luzer to eat his gefilte fish and its broth. For soup, the spoon was secondary to dipping his *challah* into the golden chicken soup and sponging it up. In went the *challah*, out came a quarter of the soup.

The meal progressed, and Izzy and Dizzy's eyes drooped lower and lower. The sound of family *zemiros* rose higher and higher. David had a beautiful voice, but he was shy. Rabbi Levi made him sit next to him and pointed out the small Hebrew words. He struggled along. Leah Levi leaned back in her chair, and Miriam snuggled closer to her.

Outside, the wind howled icily, and more snow came. But inside the Levi household it was *Shabbos*, warm and cozy. Miriam loved this time of the meal, the sleepy time, the warm safe time near her mother, watching her father's beautiful face.

But something gnawed at her underneath, bubbled up to her thoughts, bothered her. She remembered like a flash.

The Kranz house. The scary father, so mean and vicious. And the eyes, the eyes of the little girl. She was just a few houses away, but she was on another continent. So sad. So sad!

Miriam trembled with nervousness, half asleep, half awake, and her mother gave her a curious look.

I must do something, thought Miriam. But what?

3 A Surprise Meeting

IT WAS A BITTERLY FREEZING FEBRUARY. COLD, VERY COLD. IT was always cold in Toronto. It was cold in January. It was cold in May. It was cold on August nights.

Why couldn't her father have moved from New York to Miami, or Phoenix, or Rio de Janeiro? grumbled Miriam to herself as she fought her way home through the snow-banked, slippery streets. But that was not Hashem's plan. An old uncle had lived in Toronto and told her father about a teaching job in a local *cheder* school. They had come to Toronto and lived there ever since, for ten years.

Five years ago, her father had a heart attack, which ended

his teaching career. But he started his *shul*, it took root, and he stayed. People all over the city sent him donations to support his family, his study and his holy work.

Meanwhile, they were stuck in freezing Toronto. Even Izzy and Dizzy, who had comments about everything, were silent, their faces muzzled by thick scarves, as they struggled to keep up with Miriam's fast steps.

Miriam went to Bnos Chaim, the girls' school, while the boys attended Eitz Torah a few blocks away. There was always plenty of homework, and Miriam's tote bag was heavy.

The children reached the corner of Sandringham and turned down their street. The wind got a bit softer, and Miriam blew up a snow-soaked curl that tickled her forehead.

"Hello."

The children, who were bent over against the cold, looked up. Miriam's eyes widened in surprise. Her neighbor, the little Kranz girl, suddenly appeared out of the tall hedge that divided two houses. The girl stood there, looking at Miriam.

Miriam didn't know what to say. The girl had been lying in wait for her. The boys shuffled on their feet, eager to get home, out of the cold.

"Hello," answered Miriam, unsure of herself.

The girl looked at her with big, sad eyes. She was a few inches shorter than Miriam.

"Could . . . could I please talk to you for a few minutes?" she asked, haltingly.

Miriam was confused, and just a little bit scared. It was cold. It was dark. It was weird. She saw the girl dart glances back to her house, as though afraid someone might see her.

She's so afraid. The thought flashed through Miriam's head. She had no choice.

"Sure," she said.

Nervously, she blew the snowflakes out of her hair. The boys were restless behind her.

"Go home," she ordered them. "Tell Mommy I'll be home in a few minutes."

They didn't need prompting. They raced ahead homeward. Instinctively, Miriam knew what she had to do.

"Come," she whispered, and led the little girl away from the house to the safety of the corner, always making sure they were blocked from view by a bush or a tree trunk.

Miriam studied the girl. She herself was eleven, so she guessed the girl's age at nine, maybe just ten. She had dark, mousy brown hair, cut short, a gray coat and a grayish skirt. It was freezing, but she wasn't wearing either a hat or scarf.

Without asking, Miriam, who had a hood on her coat, took off her own bright striped green and white wool scarf and wrapped it around the girl's neck. The girl looked startled to be touched, but Miriam smiled reassuringly. She looked warmer already.

"We're just getting home from school now," Miriam explained, trying to find something to say. "I meet my brothers at Bathurst and Lawrence, and we take the bus together."

"I know," said the girl. She stared at the ground. "You get home every night at 5:40."

Now it was Miriam's turn to be startled. She didn't even know the time herself.

"And you leave every morning at 8:20, except when you're late and someone forgot to take lunch."

Miriam shivered a bit, but not from the cold. She must

have been watching them all the time. But why? Miriam looked at her closely, not sure, not sure at all.

"What's your name? How old are you?"

"My name is Tamara, but you can call me Tami. I'm eleven."

Eleven! She was the same age as Miriam, but she looked at least a year or two younger. Tami saw Miriam studying her, and became uncomfortable. She groped for something to say.

"I go to Armour Heights, around the corner," she said. "I'm in grade six."

"It's cold out here, Tami," Miriam suggested. "Would you like to come to my house? We can talk there."

The girl shook her head. "No, I'm not allowed to go to other people's houses. My father doesn't let me."

"What about your house? We can talk there."

Tami seemed to stiffen.

"No! No one is allowed in my house. Ever."

"Why not, Tami?"

"My father doesn't allow it. He even reads the water meter himself."

Weird, thought Miriam. Weird and sad. Miriam wanted to get away now. She wanted to go home. What did Tami want from her?

"Is it true that people come to your house to pray on Saturday morning?" she asked shyly.

"Yes. We have a little *shul* in our basement. We pray from nine to twelve, and then we have a *Kiddush*."

The girl frowned.

"*Kiddush*? What's a *Kiddush*?"

Miriam laughed. "You mean you don't know what a *Kiddush* is? Where do you come from?"

Immediately, she realized she had made a terrible mistake. Tami's face crumpled, and for a second Miriam was afraid the girl would cry. I'm an idiot, thought Miriam.

She took Tami's frozen hand, like her father did when he was explaining some deep point to a student.

"*Kiddush* is a party we have after we pray," she said. "It's great fun. We have *kugel* and fish and *chulent*. Tami, it would be great if you came. Oh, but you said your father wouldn't let you go to someone else's house."

"He won't know," answered Tami quietly. "Saturday morning is the only time I'm allowed to go out on my own to the library. My father has to let me go so I can work on projects and homework. I can sneak around the block and come around to your house from the other side. I see where people go in every Saturday."

Miriam shook herself to make sure she had heard what she thought she heard. Sneak around the block? Make up stories about going to the library? All this just to go to *shul?* Was she dreaming this? No, it was happening, right on her block, with her own neighbor.

Tami suddenly looked back nervously.

"Miriam," she said. "I have to go now. Please, could you do me a favor?"

"A favor?"

"Yes. Wait here for a moment, just in case my father is watching. He's not home, but just maybe. I don't want him to see us together. He would be very angry."

Very angry, thought Miriam. Angry for what? Talking? Saying hello?

"Tami, would he be angry with you for talking to a neighbor?"

The girl at first just looked at Miriam. Then she nodded,

the softest, saddest nod.

"I have to go," she said.

Tami took off the scarf Miriam had given her and threw it around Miriam's neck, just as Miriam had done to her a few minutes before. She gave Miriam a quick look, lifted her face up and kissed Miriam on the cheek.

Then she ran home, leaving Miriam very puzzled.

4 Shabbos Shirah

EVERY *SHABBOS* MORNING WAS A JOY FOR MIRIAM. UNLIKE Friday night, when they struggled for a *minyan*, there were always plenty of faces in the *shul*. One week was a baby-naming, another week a *Bar Mitzvah* or a *Yahrzeit Kiddush*. Then there were floaters, people who went to one *shul* this week and another the following week. It was always a question: Who would pop up this *Shabbos*? Uncle Kalman the good-hearted vegetable distributor, Rabbi Heller the bookseller and his son Chaimkel, Yitzchak the plane engineer, Morris the sad-faced, nervous stockbroker. They were all part of the Levi world.

Rabbi Levi greeted each one warmly with a "Good *Shabbos*," often before they even had time to take off their coats and boots.

Miriam loved to watch her father *Shabbos* morning. He was at peace, in his glory. All the health and money worries of the week swept away from his radiant face.

He wrapped himself in his huge black and white prayer shawl, or *tallis*, burying his head in the folds of the material for a minute, reciting special prayers. Then he adjusted it over his shoulders and back, the miniature sterling silver sea shells flowing over his neck and shoulders like waves surging on the sea shore.

Behind him, the shelves of holy *sefarim* reached to the ceiling. He reached up and brought down a volume of his precious *Chumash*. It had been printed in Poland in 1865. Each letter stood out boldly, black, black, black, as though it had been engraved on stone. On top were large letters, the words of the Torah themselves. Below, in smaller script, was Rashi's commentary, and other commentaries, and commentaries on those commentaries, smaller and smaller and smaller letters.

Miriam and her brothers took turns bringing their father cup after cup of coffee. She waited with the cup as her father ran his long fingers over the tiny words and letters. She watched his fingers walk through the words like he could feel them; his lips moved silently over each letter. His eyes followed, and she could tell when he moved down a line. When his fingers, lips and eyes paused momentarily, she knew he had reached the end of a passage.

"Tati," she whispered.

He looked up distractedly, took the cup carefully, nodded a thanks and miraculously managed not to spill a drop on the precious page of his *sefer*.

Today, Rabbi Levi was in an especially good mood. It was *Shabbos Shirah*, the *Shabbos* of Song, when the Jewish people crossed the Red Sea and Moshe Rabbeinu sang a hymn of praise.

"Did you leave out kasha for the birds?" he asked playfully. It was a custom to leave out crumbs or kasha on this *Shabbos*.

"Yes, Tati," Miriam answered. "The boys brought home bird houses from school yesterday and hung them on the back deck. We even left some *challah* for them."

"So, did the birds come? Is it gone?"

"There are no birds, Tati," Miriam sighed. "They all went to Miami where it's warm." Why couldn't they live in Miami?

Like clockwork, the congregants came, brushed themselves off, complained about the cold and found their places. At 9:15 sharp, the *davening* began.

The first part of the service went so quickly that Miriam had trouble keeping up. It was led by Mr. Goldberg, a sweet old man, with a large gnarled head topped by a fringe of white hair. He mumbled through the prayers with a thick accent, so it was hard to make out what he was saying.

Mr. Goldberg finished the first section, and then the twenty congregants waited to see who would lead the sacred *Shochen Ad* portion. Miriam was amazed. Rabbi Levi himself rose from his chair and approached the *amud*. He pulled the *tallis* even lower over his head in reverence, and began the *tefillah*.

Miriam was ecstatic. She loved her father's deep, sad voice, his Romanian *nussach* or chant and the way the words poured out with enthusiasm and heart, like a child beseeching a parent. She closed her eyes and just felt her father's prayers. My father should be more famous than he is, she thought.

The congregation had just sat down, when the door opened, allowing in the pale winter light. Miriam groaned inwardly. Through the *mechitzah*, she could see that it was Luzer. Of course, Luzer. *Shabbos Shirah* meant a special *Kiddush*, with a double portion of her mother's *chulent*, with stuffed *kishka* to boot. Luzer could smell a good *Kiddush* from five blocks away.

He took off his old coat, pulled out a worn, frazzled *tallis*, its strings twisted in every direction, nodded here and there and sat down right in front of the *mechitzah*, blocking Miriam's line of vision. His broad back, the floppy hat he insisted on wearing and his thick neck made a human wall, separating Miriam from her beloved father.

A few moments later, they heard the door upstairs open again. Now, that was odd. Usually, whoever was coming would have been here already. The pale light filtered down, and a shadow, a small, thin shadow like a bird, hesitated upstairs.

Even Rabbi Levi, deeply engrossed in the service, was curious. His head cocked a little to the side, and there was the slightest pause in the service. Everyone seemed to watch as the shadow descended slowly, and then a pair of skinny legs came into view.

Miriam stared, then shook herself awake. It was Tami! She had come! She walked down each step like it was a torture.

Miriam jumped from her place and almost knocked over the *mechitzah* as she raced up to Tami.

"Good *Shabbos*," cried Miriam. "Come, sit with me!"

She grabbed a *Siddur* from the bookshelf, pushed it into Tami's small hand and dragged her back into the women's section. Everything in the service returned to normal. The old men saw that it was just a little girl and paid no further attention.

"We're on page 294," Miriam whispered to Tami.

Tami opened the book backwards, from the left, like an English book. Miriam saw her confusion. All the numbers backwards.

"No, no," Miriam whispered. "The other way."

She closed the book, and then opened it again for Tami properly, from the right.

The *Siddur* was all in Hebrew. Tami stared down at the same page, even after the service moved on and on. She can't read a word, Miriam realized. To her, it must look like Chinese or Greek.

Tami looked at Miriam with her big eyes, looking embarrassed and ashamed. She didn't know what to do in a *shul*. Nothing. Miriam recognized that look in her eye. On *Yizkor* days, women often came to the *shul* who didn't know any Hebrew. Leah Levi had devised a system to help them, and now Miriam followed it. She set aside her own *Siddur*, took Tami's *Siddur* in her own hands and pressed even closer to her. They shared the one book, and Miriam pointed out the prayers, word by word.

The prayers were even more beautiful than usual. Miriam could tell that her father was in an elated mood. The sun had broken through, glistening off the snow banks outside, sending a glow through the room.

Everyone rose and waited for Rabbi Levi to chant the prayers aloud. Miriam waited, too. He began softly at first, then higher and higher her father's voice rose, more and more filled with the fire of the *Shabbos*, the energy and spirit of the congregation, the beauty of the day.

The *Shacharis* service ended, and then came Miriam's favorite part. Rabbi Levi turned around, his broad face and flowing beard framed by the silver border of the *tallis*, and clapped his hands together, like a king summoning his servants.

"*Kinder, aroif!* Children, come to the Torah. *Leibidick!* Quick!"

The room was packed with many children, squeezed in among the adults. They were Rabbi Levi's joy. At his command, they all broke out of the rows of chairs, and squirmed their way up to the *Aron Kodesh*, the girls running up to the *mechitzah* for a better view.

"Come on, Tami," Miriam urged, pulling her hand. But Tami was glued to her seat, too shy to stand up.

"I—I don't know what to do!" she protested.

"There's nothing to do, just watch," answered Miriam impatiently. "You don't have to know how to read. Just follow me!"

Tamara looked petrified. But Miriam had her father's impetuousness and her mother's steely determination. She yanked Tami off the seat and pushed her towards the row of girls pressed against the *mechitzah*.

They saw a crush of boys and old men, all trying to get close to the ark and Rabbi Levi. A moment later, Rabbi Levi lifted his great *Siddur* over the heads of the squirming children, then he signaled for the *Aron Kodesh* to be opened.

The velvet curtains parted and the doors opened, revealing the *shul's* treasure, the Torah scrolls. The *Ner Tamid* cast its flickering glow over the Torah mantles. The *Sifrei Torah* were squeezed as tightly together as the children who stood before them, as if they too were children.

Tami peered wide-eyed at the Torah scrolls. She seemed hypnotized by them. Each scroll had a blue mantle, with the Ten Commandments embroidered in the center, protected on each side by golden lions, their long tongues flicking red and menacing. Above and below were flowers woven out of gold thread, with hundreds of glass beads glistening like stars in the blue night sky.

The room was full of singing now. The children had all found their places and the squirming ended. Miriam stood shoulder to shoulder next to Tami and felt the holiness of the Torah flowing over both of them. Tami seemed to have forgotten herself and her shyness; she just stared and stared, like a thirsty person drinking in pitcher after pitcher of cold water.

The singing ended and then came yet another pleasant surprise for Miriam. Usually, the weekly lesson was read from the large, newer Torah that had been donated two years before. But Miriam's father pointed to a small Torah that stood on the right. It was almost a third smaller than the other scrolls, and the mantle was simpler. But it was Rabbi Levi's own Torah, the one he had brought with him from Romania. It was the only remnant of his whole family, of a world which was now no more. It was very precious, very valuable, very special.

Mr. Goldberg carefully lifted out the Torah and handed it to Miriam's father. He kissed it like a father kissing a child, held it against his great chest and began the procession around the room. It was crowded, noisy and merry as the press of children and elders followed. A dozen hands reached out to touch the Torah with their fingers or with the corner of a *Siddur*. Then Rabbi Levi hugged the Torah even more tightly, his eyes closed with joy and emotion.

Tami stood pressed against the *mechitzah* for the duration of the *davening*. Her brow set in concentration, she watched every move Rabbi Levi made. All too soon, the service reached its conclusion.

The delicious aroma of the bubbling *chulent* wafted down from the kitchen. *Kiddush* was coming, and everyone grew restless and hungry. The two *Kiddush* tables were laid out like a letter T. The children herded around the back table, at the top of the T, while Miriam's father stood at the bottom of the T with the adults. It was very crowded. Rabbi Levi lifted the great silver goblet and recited the *Kiddush*. Then the grabbing began. Wine in styrofoam cups, crackers, cookies, herring, pieces of gefilte fish, homemade cakes, paper plates and plastic forks flew from hand to hand.

Miriam had the job of helping her mother bring down the huge pot of *chulent* that had simmered all night on the stove. Every Friday afternoon, Leah Levi prepared meat, potatoes, beans and spices, set a low flame, and then prayed for the best. It was a Jewish time bomb, a *chulent* time bomb, set to go off at noon on *Shabbos*, and it was delicious.

Leah Levi held the pot carefully with two hand towels, while Miriam followed carrying a huge ladle to dole out the *chulent*. Tami followed closely behind her.

As they entered the room, Luzer bounded over to Mrs. Levi, standing like a wolf in front of a lamb chop.

"And here's the *chulent*!" announced Luzer. His huge greasy hat bobbed with excitement. "Ummm, I just love that smell!"

Without waiting for an invitation, he lifted the lid off the *chulent* pot, wafting a cloud of steam into the room. Luzer breathed deeply, his eyes closed in pleasure.

"It's cold outside," he said. "I deserve doubles!"

"Doubles for Luzer and doubles for everyone!" cried Miriam playfully.

She ladled a piping hot portion onto Tami's plate and gave her a wink. For the first time since Miriam had met her, Tami smiled. Her eyes crinkled with humor, and her cheeks squeezed into two thin, pretty dimples.

She's so pretty, thought Miriam to herself. If she would only dress right and fix her hair, she could be so beautiful.

5 Super Student

A STRANGE, STRANGE FRIENDSHIP BEGAN BETWEEN MIRIAM and Tami.

Miriam never knew when she would see Tami next. She was very close or very far. She could disappear for a *Shabbos* or two, then come to *shul*. Miriam spotted her during the week, always at a distance. She would wave, even call out, but Tami acted as though she didn't see her.

It seemed to Miriam that Tami was very scared, afraid that her father was watching her every step. There was another thing that was creepy. Whenever Miriam and the boys walked past Tami's house on the way home from school,

Miriam slowed her pace just a bit. Izzy and Dizzy were too busy talking about some hockey or baseball game to notice, but Miriam used the extra few seconds to subtly scan the windows.

I can't see her, but I know Tami is watching me, Miriam thought. Where is she hiding? She's always watching me.

And then, out of the blue, Tami would suddenly appear on *Shabbos* morning, as though nothing had happened. Miriam's mother took a deep, kind interest in the strange girl but wisely did not ask too many questions.

Miriam had never discussed Tami with her father. She didn't want to disturb him when he was learning or talking to the people who depended upon him for his wisdom and knowledge. She didn't want to burden him with problems. So Tami would come and go from the *shul* each week, and Miriam was never sure whether her father had even noticed her.

One *Shabbos* morning, everything changed. Rabbi Levi made *Kiddush* as usual and was settled in his seat surrounded by his congregants, when he suddenly pointed his finger at Tami, beckoning her to him.

Tami looked at Miriam uncertainly. She is afraid of him, thought Miriam. Without asking, she took Tami gently by the hand and led her to her father.

"*Good Shabbos*," greeted Rabbi Levi. "I see you like our little *shul*."

Tami just stared at him. She squeezed Miriam's hand harder, and Miriam squeezed back lightly, reassuringly.

"Did you have anything to eat? Cake? Gefilte fish?"

Tami nodded.

"Where do you go to school?" pressed Rabbi Levi. "Do you go to Hebrew school?"

Miriam knew her father was trying to be kind and friendly, but she was afraid his powerful voice and sharp direct questions would frighten Tami away. And what would happen if he discovered she was their strange neighbor's daughter? He might pepper her with questions and unwittingly embarrass her.

"I don't go to Hebrew school," Tami finally answered.

Rabbi Levi looked to Miriam, as though expecting an explanation. Miriam watched his eyebrows. Would they go up? That would mean trouble. No, they bunched up merrily, and a twinkle came to Rabbi Levi's eye. He understands, sighed Miriam with relief.

"You don't go to Hebrew school, and yet you come to *shul*, *Shabbos* after *Shabbos*. What a beautiful little *neshamah* you have. What a Jewish *neshamah*! Miriam, are you asleep? Such a nice friend, and she doesn't know Hebrew? What is your name?"

"Tami."

"Good. Tami, I am hiring a teacher to teach you to read. How would you like that?"

Tami looked at Miriam, almost in panic.

"Who?" queried Miriam.

"You," announced Rabbi Levi firmly. "You, Miriam. I am appointing you to teach this lovely girl Hebrew. Of course, I cannot discuss salary on *Shabbos*, but you will be well taken care of, I promise." He turned to Tami. "Don't look so frightened, Tami. Do you know what I see in your eyes?"

Tami shook her head.

"I see the letters of the Torah dancing in your eyes. Look!" He waved his hand gently before her eyes. "Look, I pulled out a Hebrew letter. See, it was there all the time! Now go back and enjoy your *chulent*."

Miriam and Tami looked at each other and smiled. The girls raced to the safety of the back table, where Leah Levi still doled out second portions of *chulent.*

"Nu," she asked, "how did your conversation go with Tati?"

Miriam eyed her mother, who avoided eye contact. So she had been behind the whole thing! It was all planned. But it had worked. Tati's directness had broken the ice and Tami seemed relieved. The opportunity to learn Hebrew had finally come her way.

But teaching Tami was not simple. It was wonderful, it was sad, it was an ordeal, it was strange.

Tami could not openly visit the Levi home, or she would be in very big trouble. Her father must never see her with Miriam, or she might be severely punished.

Shabbos morning, tutoring was impossible. There was no time during services and too much noise, and when Izzy and Dizzy were around, it was impossible to accomplish anything.

They developed a secret plan. Tami had entered a new term, with heavier assignments. Her teacher insisted on her students working on library projects. Her father had to let her out two afternoons a week. Once a week, she left the library early, sneaked around the block and came down to the Levi basement. She moved swiftly, hiding behind trees and bushes, so that her father wouldn't spot her. After the lesson, she circled her way back.

At each lesson, Miriam and Tami quickly opened the brown Hebrew reader. There was no time to talk. Tami had to leave in fifteen minutes. The recollection of the violent face of Mr. Kranz loomed over them, and sometimes Miriam shivered, remembering how it looked so close to hers.

The first lesson held surprises for them both. Miriam pointed to the large black letters in the reader and named each in turn.

"*Aleph, bais, gimel, daled*," began Miriam.

"*Aleph, bais, gimel, daled*," repeated Tami.

Next, Miriam named the vowels and showed Tami how to put them together with each letter. That was all Miriam had to do. Tami caught on immediately, and went racing down the page on her own. In a few minutes, she was ready for the next set of letters.

"*Hay, vav, zayin, ches*," Miriam pointed out.

Tami wouldn't let her finish. She rattled off the letters, blended in the new vowels, read the old and new letters together, the new sounds, the old sounds. Sharp, clear, precise.

"Lesson Three," the page read. Miriam couldn't believe it. Lesson Three in fifteen minutes.

"Maybe we're going too fast," Miriam suggested. "I don't want to mix you up."

"But it's so easy. Let's go on, please!" demanded Tami.

So they covered yet a few more letters, as much as they could do in the few minutes left. Miriam had never met a student like Tami before. She had helped a few younger children, but Tami was like a starving person gobbling down bite after bite, swallowing, swallowing, hungry for the slightest crumb. After the lesson, Tami carefully stuffed the reader into her bag under some other books. Miriam didn't ask, but she understood. If Mr. Kranz discovered it, who knew what would happen?

The lessons continued into April. They were wonderful, but the dark threat of Tami's father hung over them like a terrifying storm cloud. Miriam could still recall that day when she stumbled into the Kranz house. She could still feel the heat of Mr. Kranz's rapid, angry breathing. He invaded Miriam's sleep. She often dreamt of being trapped in her basement, with Mr. Kranz after her, gripping some weapon (she wasn't sure what) in his hand. And her cowardly brothers, Izzy and Dizzy, just watched the whole scene through the window, doing nothing to help her!

For me it is just a nightmare and I'm scared even though I'm safe, thought Miriam. But for Tami, it is real life. What must she be going through?

Tami never spoke about her father, nor did Miriam intrude on her home life. She was afraid to. Tami was like a delicate flower, fragile and thin, who might break if pressed too hard.

It wasn't fair. It just wasn't fair.

Miriam loved Tami. She was like a little sister, although Tami was actually a little older. Miriam had heard about children who were abused by their parents. Whenever they were together, Miriam could sense whether Tami had just been through another angry scene with her father. It was in her eyes. Sometimes she would come to a lesson, and her eyes looked like they had a veil over them, as if she were far, far away.

I must tell someone, Miriam promised herself. There was only one person she could ever tell—her mother. But she knew her mother would tell her father, and then there would be an explosion. He would turn red with fury and his blood pressure would rise. He would throw on his big black hat, stomp down the front stairs and bang on the Kranz door, demanding an explanation.

Rabbi Levi was a quiet, loving, gentle man, but when he was angry, he was all Romanian. He might even have a second heart attack, Heaven forbid. He might even . . .

No, Miriam dare not risk it, or that horrible man might avenge himself against her not only in a dream but in real life as well. All she could do was squeeze Tami's hand a little harder, look a little longer and deeper into her sad eyes and try to send her a mind message: "I know what's happening. I care."

After four weeks, Tami mastered all the letters and vowels and was sounding out words. She was very frustrated. She tried to follow the *Shabbos davening*, but the leader read very fast. Zoom, zoom, vroom! A hundred kilometers an hour. Even Miriam had trouble keeping up, so what could Tami do?

At the start of the fifth lesson, Miriam was about to open the reader, when Tami leaned her hand on it, holding it closed.

"Miriam," she pleaded. "I know how to read now. The reader is too easy. Please teach me from the *Siddur*."

There was an old *Siddur* with large black letters on the bookshelf above them. Miriam reached up and laid it on the table in front of them.

"Let's start with *Adon Olam*," suggested Miriam. It was a simple hymn, an easy melody that everyone knew. They started together, Miriam easily, Tami tripping over the new words, new phrases. The longer the song continued, the more she struggled; and the more Miriam grew impatient, the quicker she sang.

Suddenly, Tami burst into tears and put the *Siddur* down on the table.

"I can't sing so fast! I can't sing so fast," she cried, raising her voice in anger.

Miriam's mother, alerted by the shouting downstairs,

opened the upstairs door from the kitchen.

"Miriam," she shouted down the steps. "Is everything all right?"

Tami quickly quieted. There was a second's silence.

"It's nothing," Miriam called back. "We were just singing." After all, they *had* been singing. That was no lie.

There was an eerie silence. Miriam knew what was happening. Her mother was waiting at the door upstairs, listening, waiting. She knew Miriam could not always be fully believed. How does she always know? wondered Miriam. There must be something in my voice. Miriam looked at Tami and put her finger over her lips. They waited out her mother. A few more seconds. Finally, the door shut.

"Why did you get so upset?" Miriam demanded of Tami in a voice just above a whisper. "If you wanted me to go slower, I would have gone slower. I'm your friend, Tami. You didn't have to cry."

Tami recovered and looked ashamed.

"I—I know. But I want so much to learn these songs, to be able to follow in the *Siddur*."

"But you will, I promise."

"No, I won't, Miriam," Tami answered sharply.

"You won't? Why not?"

"It's no use. It will all stop. You will stop. You will get tired of me. You won't teach me. You won't let me in your home. I just know. It will all be taken away from me."

Miriam stared at her. She didn't know what to say. It was crazy! What kind of world did Tami live in, that nothing good could ever happen to her? Was no one ever nice to her? Did no one ever care for her? Did no parent ever kiss her, hold her?

Miriam was about to shout back, but she caught her

breath. She spoke quietly, as her mother would to her.

"Tami, you are my friend. I love you. I really do. I love teaching you. I'm not going to throw you out, ever. Do you understand? You are my friend. You are my student, even if it takes us twenty years."

Their eyes met, and there was silence.

"Pick up the *Siddur*, and let's do *Adon Olam* again," Miriam ordered.

But Tami just continued staring. Finally, she picked up the *Siddur*, leaned over and kissed Miriam on the cheek.

"Quit fussing and sing," demanded Miriam with mock strictness.

The lesson continued.

6 The Missing Piece

THE SUN ROSE HIGHER AND HIGHER IN THE APRIL SKY, AND the birds returned to their homes among the backyard branches. The old men returned from Miami, their skins tanned, their hair bleached whiter by the sun. The melting snow seeped in, causing a flood in the synagogue basement.

After the terrible winter frost, the whole world came alive again, and *Pesach* was just around the corner. The Levi house stirred and whirred with excitement.

Leah Levi was busy cleaning out shelves and stocking up on food, and the children were learning commentaries on the *Haggadah* to recite at the *Seder* table. Downstairs, a steady stream of visitors knocked on the side door and went down to the *shul* to sell their *chametz*.

Rabbi Levi looked forward to these few weeks the whole winter. He had accumulated bills at the bakery, the butcher shop and the grocery. Now a small flood of cash came in. As people left after the ritual of selling *chametz*, they wished him a happy and *kosher Pesach* and shook his hand, slipping into the handshake folded bills—tens, twenties, occasionally a fifty or even a hundred. It was money the family needed like a bone-dry plant needed water.

The Levis always had guests for the *Seder*. David the folk singer was away, but Leah Levi met a young woman in the supermarket who had never been at a *Seder* in her life, and Leah insisted that she come for the first *Seder* together with her seven-year-old daughter. Leah did not even have to consult her husband. She knew he would approve.

Miriam wanted to invite Tami, but she knew it was impossible. She hinted, of course. She mentioned the *Seder* a few times, and one time mentioned how great it would be if Tami could come. But Tami just looked back with those big, sad eyes, and an invisible veil went over them. Miriam did not ask again.

It was the evening before *Pesach*. Miriam, Izzy and Dizzy busied themselves in the kitchen, wrapping ten pieces of bread carefully in aluminum foil. Each child was given a few pieces to hide around the house, so their father could find them during *Bedikas Chametz*. No one told the other where he hid his pieces, and Rabbi Levi had no idea at all, so that his search would be a sincere one.

The sun set, and night came quickly. The phone was taken off the hook to avoid interruptions. Izzy gathered the candle, feather and wooden spoon. Dizzy made a nuisance of himself, demanding to know when their father would come up from the *shul* and begin the search. To make matters worse, Izzy had broken the sidepiece of his glasses, and they kept slipping down his thin nose.

Izzy was being Izzy, and Dizzy was being Dizzy.

Just as three stars twinkled in the night sky, Miriam's father came up the stairs, dressed in his long black coat and hat, and prepared to begin the search. He gave Dizzy a sharp look to calm him, took the *Siddur* from Miriam and held the candle in his hand.

The house lights were shut. Miriam wondered at the change. They were no longer on Sandrigham Drive, but a thousand miles away or a hundred years ago. The candlelight made their faces glow like in a painting.

Rabbi Levi looked at his wife with a soft smile. Miriam could tell her father was very happy to embark on this great *mitzvah*, a *mitzvah* that could only be performed once a year. Leah Levi smiled back and nodded. Miriam understood that they were speaking to each other with their eyes, but she did not quite understand what they were saying.

He opened his great black *Siddur*, and recited the *berachah*.

Rabbi Levi put down the *Siddur*, handed the candle to Miriam and took the feather and spoon in his hands. The *Bedikas Chametz*, the annual search for the least bit of crumbs, began.

Silence reigned, except for an occasional tussle between Izzy and Dizzy over who would stand closer to their father or whose turn it was to hold the paper bag where the *chametz* pieces were to be placed.

The search was not merely symbolic. Rabbi Levi was looking for *chametz*, any *chametz*, anywhere in his possession—under the breakfront and under the couch, behind dressers, in closets, stuck at the bottom of the refrigerator, in the *shul*, in the garage, in the basement, under the children's beds.

To Miriam, he looked like a detective searching for fingerprints. He bent over closely, while she held the candle just a few inches before his face. Nothing was too small for his attention. It was slow, careful and tedious, and then at last, Rabbi Levi hit on one of the prepared pieces of *chametz*. He joyously pushed it onto the big wooden spoon with the edge of the feather. His eyes shone with the *mitzvah*.

Meanwhile, Izzy and Dizzy went crazy.

"Bingo!" they shouted and began jumping and cheering.

Rabbi Levi gave them a sharp look for talking during this sacred moment. His eyes clearly said, "*Nu!* We're in the middle of a *mitzvah!*"

They calmed down. The search continued, through the dining room, living room, kitchen, breakfast room, up the hall stairs, from bedroom to bedroom.

Bingo! Another *chametz* piece was found, this time in Miriam's closet. Miriam was annoyed. She didn't care for anyone to go into her room without asking.

The little parade silently marched down into the basement synagogue. Rabbi Levi was especially concerned with the small closet underneath the stairs. That was where the crackers were kept for *Kiddush*.

Nothing could stop Miriam's father once he had a mind to do something. Even the possibility of the candle setting the closet afire did not deter him. He pushed his great bulk deep into the small closet until he looked like he was trapped in it. Suddenly, he pulled himself out of the closet and held something up triumphantly. It was a cracker! He quickly motioned for the spoon and feather and swept every crumb of the *chametz* out. He was ecstatic.

It took almost an hour and a half, but the whole house was searched. There was a small treasure of the collected pieces, the cracker and its crumbs, the feather, spoon and the brown paper bag. Rabbi Levi placed it carefully on the kitchen table, opened the bag and pulled out the pieces without spilling any crumbs.

"Four . . . five . . . six . . . seven . . . eight . . . nine . . . nine . . . nine . . ."

He reached in deeper and then shook the bag. His face turned pale.

"Where is the missing piece?" he demanded. "What happened to it?"

"My pieces are there," said Miriam quickly. There was a storm coming, she knew.

"You found all my pieces," chimed in Izzy, his glasses skiing dramatically down his nose. "I remember where I put them, and you got all of them."

Everyone looked at Dizzy.

"Dizzy, where is your last piece?"

He looked like he wanted to escape.

"You have them all," he answered defiantly.

"No, we don't," said his mother firmly. "Dizzy, think! Where is it?"

Dizzy shrugged and put out his hands helplessly.

"I don't know . . ." he whined. "I can't remember everything! Am I the Vilna Gaon? It's somewhere!"

"Somewhere!" Rabbi Levi exploded. "The night before *Pesach*, and the *chametz* is . . . *somewhere*?"

"Dizzy, can't you ever get anything straight?" Miriam

shouted. "You always forget everything. You're going to forget your head someday."

So, Dizzy proceeded to do what Dizzy always did under the circumstances, the final defense. He let out a wail. Once he was bawling, there was no way of talking to him anymore.

Rabbi Levi groaned, and his wife tried to calm him. It was dangerous for him to get too excited. She turned to Dizzy and spoke very calmly.

"Dizzy, we're not angry. We're just trying to find the missing piece. Now try to remember where you put it."

Dizzy calmed to a sniffling whimper.

"I don't know. I put them in my back pocket, and then I took them out and . . ."

As he spoke, he reached into his pocket and out came the missing piece!

"*Baruch Hashem*," cried Rabbi Levi. "*Baruch Hashem*!"

"I can't believe it," muttered Miriam. "You're such a bubblehead that you never even put it out. How could Tati find it then? There were no ten pieces!"

"Oh, be quiet," he shot back at Miriam. "You're not in charge."

And then, to prove his point, he hit Izzy. The boys began a shoving match, Miriam tried to separate them and Rabbi Levi joyously turned the page of the *Siddur* to "*Kol Chamira*."

7 A Special Gift

IT WAS THE AFTERNOON BEFORE THE *SEDER*. MIRIAM AND HER mother returned from some last minute shopping. Rabbi Levi and the boys were away baking special "*mitzvah matzos*," round *matzos* rolled by hand and baked to a dark brown crisp. The afternoon quiet was a pleasure after the last minute excitement of burning the *chametz* in the morning and the preparation for the *Seder* to come. Leah Levi and Miriam passed through the living room and stopped in their tracks. Luzer the Shmoozer was stretched out like a whale on the couch. He grinned when he saw them.

"Luzer," demanded Mrs. Levi. "What are you doing here? Who let you in?"

He pulled himself up slowly.

"I came in on my own. The door wasn't locked."

Leah Levi gasped at him open-mouthed, so he gave her a little lecture.

"Well, Rebbitzen, doesn't the *Haggadah* say that all who are hungry should come and eat? Well, I'm hungry, and you and the Rebbe are my nicest friends. So here I am. And to tell you the truth, one couldn't find a finer family or a better cook."

Miriam looked at her astonished mother, and her mother looked at her. Miriam knew how tired her mother was and how she had resolved not to invite anyone to the *Seder* beside the young woman and her daughter.

Yet, here's Luzer!

Miriam wished she had the *chutzpah* to ask him to find someplace else, just this once, but she didn't. It would be a bad thing to do.

"Where's Tati?" fumed Mrs. Levi, storming into the kitchen and putting down their packages. "Where is Tati whenever I need him?"

Like an actor on cue, Rabbi Levi marched into the house happily, carrying a large brown package of freshly baked *matzos*, Izzy and Dizzy frisking behind him.

"Good *Erev Yom Tov*," he greeted the house joyously. Then he saw his wife's face, noticed Luzer wandering in the dining room, put two and two together and sighed.

"Don't say anything," he whispered to his wife, even before he put down the package. "I'll help. It's *Pesach*, and he has no place else. Come, give me the horseradish, get me the nuts and apples for *charoses*. Don't worry, I'll help, Leah, and the boys . . ." He turned to Izzy and Dizzy desperately. "You'll help your mother, yes, boys?" He was talking very fast, like a man in great trouble.

"I'll help," chimed in Izzy, sensing duty.

"Me, too," echoed Dizzy, sensing danger.

Mrs. Levi was staring at them icily. It was like the barometer plunging before a tornado.

Mrs. Levi sighed. What could she do? You couldn't embarrass another person. You couldn't throw Luzer out. She caught her breath, tried to smile and gave everyone directions.

The *Seder* table glowed.

Rabbi Levi sat at the head of the table, dressed in a gleaming white *kittel*. He leaned heavily on a large pillow encased in an embroidered white cover. With his white yarmulke, his white, flowing beard, white robes, white pillow, his sparkling eyes, he looked to Miriam like an angel.

On his right sat Leah, Miriam, Pattie Stone and her daughter Jill. Across from them were Izzy, Dizzy and hulking over them all, Luzer the Shmoozer.

Miriam loved when her father told the *Pesach* story of slavery, suffering and redemption. He spoke about Egypt, but she knew he was really speaking about himself. He, too, had once been a slave, to the Nazis in Europe. He never spoke about those days, not openly.

But now a look came over her father's face when he spoke about the cruelty of the ancient Egyptians, how they searched out every Jewish male child for slaughter, how babies were hidden, of forced labor and starvation. She knew he was talking not only about the ancient days but about what he had seen, the destruction of his family. Over and over he chanted the words, ". . . In every generation they rise against us to destroy us! In every generation . . . to destroy us . . ."

And then he turned to Miriam, Izzy and Dizzy.

"Remember, children," he said. "We must always be vigilant. We are surrounded by enemies, and we don't know who they are."

"But we also have friends, Mordechai," Leah interjected. "Not everyone is an enemy. Not everyone hates."

Rabbi Levi looked blankly at her for a moment, lost in his thoughts. He went on without answering.

Finally, the story ended, the second cup was drunk, and the meal was about to begin. Luzer, who seemed to be in hibernation during the long reading, woke up and almost jigged with excitement.

Rabbi Levi held the two whole *matzos* high, closed his eyes and recited the *berachos*. He leaned back and carefully bit into the pieces. His eyes were far away, thinking. About what? wondered Miriam. She could never know. Then he handed out *matzoh* to everyone.

With hand motions, Rabbi Levi indicated to Luzer to lean, but Luzer was having trouble leaning. He looked like a bear struggling over a bone, bending over hard to break through the wood-dry *matzoh*.

The bitter horseradish was tasted, the Hillel sandwich of yet more *matzoh* and *maror* was distributed, and the meal began.

Fish was served, big lumps of warm gefilte fish that Miriam helped her mother shape earlier. Luzer smacked his lips, ate three pieces and attacked another piece of *matzoh*. Miriam and her mother watched him from the corners of their eyes. Luzer was in *matzoh* heaven, and there was no bringing him down.

Actually, Luzer was eating for three. Pattie and Jill were so shy that they nibbled like birds. No wonder she's so slim and graceful, thought Miriam.

"Eat, eat!" Leah Levi kept urging them. "Eat!"

"It's a *mitzvah*," added Rabbi Levi.

He kept passing the girl more pieces of *matzoh*, and there was a little pile of crumbs in front of her.

Meanwhile, every *gematria* and *Medrash* Izzy and Dizzy had learned for the last month came bubbling up from them. Izzy would start and then Dizzy would protest.

"Hey, that's my *dvar Torah*! I'm supposed to say that."

"Is not!"

"Is so!"

Rabbi Levi rolled his eyes upwards and listened patiently. Miriam took charge.

"No, it's *my* turn now," she said.

The boys calmed down. Miriam calmly explained a passage from the *Haggadah*. Everyone listened. Order was restored. The boys knew that if they interrupted, Miriam would get them later, *Pesach* or not.

Luzer was truly amazing. Miriam expected to see him eat the tablecloth. In a wink he had downed three pieces of gefilte fish, two and a half bowls of soup, half a chicken, and eight . . . nine macaroons, two glasses of Slivovitz and *matzoh, matzoh, matzoh*.

Miriam knew she wasn't the only one counting. Izzy and Dizzy had secret bets on how much he would eat and how many cups he would drink and how many times he would add, "Ah, that *schmecks* of *Gan Eden*."

Miriam lost count.

It grew late, and Rabbi Levi rushed to eat the *afikomen*. But he had to negotiate first. Izzy and Dizzy, along with the shy little girl Jill, had stolen the *afikomen* from underneath Rabbi Levi's pillow. The boys snatched it easily every year, because their father hid it there every year.

Rabbi Levi made a short play of trying to find the *matzoh* in his pillow. He turned to the boys.

"Well, boys, where is the *afikomen?*"

"What will you give us?" demanded Dizzy, before Izzy even had a chance to open his mouth.

"What do you want?"

"Could I get one of those new Uncle Fendel tapes at Sefer Tov Book Store?"

Rabbi Levi looked to his wife. He had no idea what these things cost. She nodded yes.

"Fine. And you, Dizzy?"

"I want a baseball glove!"

"You have a baseball glove already, Dizzy," interrupted his mother.

"But you bought that used in the thrift shop," argued Dizzy. "I always have baseball gloves from the thrift shop. Izzy is getting a new tape, isn't he? So I want to get a *new* glove."

"That's a good *sevara*," answered Rabbi Levi appreciatively. He liked good reasoning whether it was in Talmud or baseball gloves. He agreed.

The boys pulled out the *matzoh* from where it had been bulging under Izzy's jacket and handed it to their father. They returned to their places happily.

"Wait," ordered Rabbi Levi before proceeding. "Didn't the little girl help you hide the *afikomen?*"

On hearing this, the child hid shyly behind her mother's arm, clinging to her.

"Sure she did," answered Dizzy.

"Well, where is she?" demanded Rabbi Levi. "Come here, er . . ."

"Jill," whispered Leah Levi to her husband.

"How do you say it?" asked Rabbi Levi, struggling with the J sound.

"Jill, please come here."

The girl rose reluctantly.

"Go," her mother urged in a sharp whisper.

She made the long walk around the table until she was beside Rabbi Levi, looking up at the great waterfall of white beard.

"Would you like a present?" he asked.

She nodded imperceptibly.

"For you, I have two presents," said Rabbi Levi, smiling warmly. "First, we will get you a doll. Would you like a doll?"

"She's too old for dolls, Mordechai," Leah whispered. "Get her a game. We can pick it up when we buy Dizzy his glove."

"Fine!" He accepted the correction. "A game! Would you like a game?"

Jill nodded more confidently.

"But I have a special gift for you," Rabbi Levi continued. "An even bigger gift. Your mother told me that you never received a proper Jewish name. Do you know your Jewish name?"

Jill shook her head. Miriam was sure the girl didn't understand what her father was talking about.

"Of course you don't know your Jewish name, because you don't have one," said Rabbi Levi. "But I am going to give you one right downstairs, in our own *shul*. Would you like that?"

"What will it be, Tati?" asked Miriam.

"Aha!" beamed Rabbi Levi. "That will be our secret. We will choose a beautiful name, a holy name. I have one in mind already. Do you know what?"

The little girl shook her head.

"I will give you a hint." Rabbi Levi swung out his arm like a bee flying.

"Z-z-z-z," he hissed.

The little girl looked at her mother, not sure what to make of all this. Rabbi Levi smiled.

"Go back to your seat, *shainkeit*," he said. "We are going to do something very great before *Shavuos* comes."

Rabbi Levi beamed, and for a second, a far away look fell over his eyes. The girl ran back to the safety of the seat near her mother, and the *Seder* continued.

Now came the part Miriam loved most. A huge silver goblet stood in the middle of the table, glowing in the lights of the candles, reflecting the multicolored flower bouquet that grazed it.

"Fill the cup of Eliyahu," ordered Rabbi Levi.

Leah carefully poured the purple wine from the crystal decanter into the cup. She handed the cup to her husband. He rose heavily, balancing the huge cup in his large hand, and gestured to Miriam.

"*Shainkeit*, go open the door for our honored guest."

Miriam took little Jill by the hand, and together they walked to the outside door which could be seen from the dining room table. She opened the door wide, letting in the cool night air. High above, the stars twinkled. It was a magical night.

"Rise, children, rise!" ordered Rabbi Levi. "Rise to greet the honored guest!"

There was a shuffle of chairs, and a little wind blew in,

ruffling Miriam's hair, as though Eliyahu Hanavi had passed by her.

Miriam's father raised his voice, waking her from her reverie.

"*Shfoch chamascha . . .*"

Rabbi Levi held his large *Haggadah* in his hand, but Miriam could tell he was not reading. He was speaking, speaking to Eliyahu Hanavi, sending a message to Hashem's throne.

There was a pause, and Rabbi Levi caught his breath. He looked around, and peace returned to his face.

Miriam peered out the door, to see if any neighbors could hear them. She was afraid the family was too noisy, and the neighbors might complain. She peered down the street, craning her neck.

What was that? A shade slammed down in Tamara's house, just as she looked in that direction. Then the light went out. But Miriam knew what she had seen. Had Tamara been watching her house all the time, all night? Was it her crazy father? She stared harder. Was someone staring back in the darkness? Should she wave? Was it her imagination?

There was a tap on her shoulder, and Miriam jumped. It was her mother.

"Miriam, didn't you hear us? Please close the door." Miriam closed the door tightly, and her mother hugged her. "My big girl, you must be so tired."

She led Miriam back to the table. Miriam wanted to close her eyes and go to sleep. Something was happening in that house that she didn't like, didn't understand. Was she going crazy? She felt Tami talking to her, even now. She heard her voice in her ears.

"Help me, Miriam . . . Help me, Miriam . . ."

She clung tightly to her mother as the *Seder* continued. Miriam sang along, even though her eyes drooped. Her father joked a little with her, and the wine she had tasted made her feel warm.

But inside, a part of her was frightened.

8 A Secret Rendezvous

TAMARA HAD DISAPPEARED: SHE NEVER RETURNED TO TAKE lessons. Well, not actually disappeared. Miriam twice spotted her scurrying into her house, like a mouse into its hole. But something was wrong. From a distance, Tamara looked so sad, so fragile and skinny.

What was happening in the Kranz house?

I am a coward, confessed Miriam to herself. All I have to do—what I should do—is go the Kranz house, knock on the door and ask for Tamara.

But she was very afraid of Tami's weird, cruel father.

Miriam also knew that she was attached to Tamara with

an invisible cord. She thought about Tami all the time, and she knew Tami was thinking about her.

"Hello, Tami," Miriam whispered into the air, letting the words float over the rooftops and into Tamara's bedroom.

"Where is your little friend, the one you are teaching how to *daven*?" asked Miriam's father one day.

"She hasn't been in touch," Miriam admitted.

"What a pity," sighed Rabbi Levi. "She's a nice little girl. I had hopes for her."

Should Miriam say something? Tell the whole story? Upset her father? No, she would wait.

Five weeks after *Pesach* even Toronto had warmed up a bit. Trees budded, birds flitted after each other, Blue Jay pitchers replaced Maple Leaf goalies, the sun sparkled.

Miriam walked home from school with her brothers. They argued about how fast a certain Blue Jay pitcher threw the ball.

"Miriam!" someone whispered.

Miriam kept walking, not sure she heard anything.

"Miriam!" The whisper was louder, clearer.

The boys looked around. There was no one.

"Who is that?" asked Izzy, adjusting his glasses.

Miriam knew who it was, although she didn't see anyone.

"Go home, boys," she ordered.

"Miriam, there's someone calling your name. Maybe it's Hashem, like with Shmuel Hanavi."

"Go home right now, boys," she hissed at them.

They looked at her strangely, saw her face tighten and didn't ask questions. They ran home.

Miriam turned and calculated where Tamara must be hiding. She walked around a tall evergreen bush. When she saw Tami, she was stunned. The little girl cowered behind the branches, her eyes wide. She looked like someone from the newspapers, a refugee or an abandoned child. She had on a ghastly flowered dress that even the thrift shop would refuse. Tami's thin arms poked out of her short sleeves like two sticks.

Miriam hugged her, not saying anything at first. She felt so bad, so mad at herself. Why hadn't she pursued Tami? Why had she been such a coward?

"Where have you been?" she finally blurted, imitating Tami's whisper.

"Nowhere. I was nowhere."

"Why didn't you come back to our *shul*? Even my father asked for you."

Tamara pulled back from Miriam's embrace and stared her in the face. She looked like a person confessing.

"I was caught."

"Caught? Caught doing what?"

"My father caught me. You remember Passover night, when you opened the front door? It was late."

Miriam's face clouded deeply. She knew what was coming, like a train heading straight for her head.

"I locked myself in the bathroom so I could watch your house. I could see your table through the window." She tried to smile. "You didn't know . . ."

Miriam shook her head dumbly, speechless.

"I was looking for you. I so much wanted to see you, Miriam. And then you opened the door and looked right at me!"

Tamara's eyes grew wider, reflecting her excitement, her pleasure.

"But I forgot . . ." Deep gloom, fear, fright cascaded over her pale eyes.

"Forgot what?"

Tami fell silent.

"Forgot what?" demanded Miriam angrily.

She took Tamara's small hand in hers. It was cold. Miriam touched her face tenderly. Tami closed her eyes like a cat, and the words tumbled out of her quickly.

"I forgot how long I had been in the bathroom. My father started pounding on the door, just pounding and pounding. Bang! Bang! Bang! He screamed at me, 'Get out of there! What are you doing? Who are you watching?' "

Tami lowered her eyes and began to tremble.

"Miriam, he broke through the door! I heard the wood split, and I saw his fist. It was all splintered and bloody! I was so ashamed . . ."

"Ashamed?" heaved Miriam. "What did you have to be ashamed of? What did you do wrong?"

She shook Tamara by her shoulders, but the elfin girl just wept, refusing to accept Miriam's words. Between breaths she could only mumble, "Ashamed . . . Ashamed . . ."

Miriam let go of her, and both girls calmed down in silence.

"That's why I didn't come back. My father knows I like you, that I want to be like you. He watches me like a hawk now. I have to explain everything I do, everywhere I go.

"But I think I can sneak away this Saturday. We have three projects to do for school. My father has to let me go out this Saturday to the library. I must have extra time to work, and I can try to come some of the time to you. Is that okay?"

Miriam looked at her, hardly able to answer. She nodded, very firmly.

"But I may have to come late," she said. "And leave in the middle. Do you think your father will be angry at me? I like your father so much, I wouldn't want him to be mad at me."

Miriam reassured her and tried to smile. She felt so sad, so bad, so mad at herself, at Tamara's father, even at her own parents. Couldn't someone help?

Tamara backed off, making way for the dangerous run home, hoping her father had not seen her. But before she retreated, she stopped and gazed into Miriam's eyes.

"Oh, Miriam, how I wish we were sisters. How I wish your parents were my parents, that we could share a room and have neat posters on the wall and listen to tapes and hug each other when we're afraid in the dark . . ."

"You *are* my sister," blurted Miriam impulsively. "We are secret sisters. We're always together, right?"

Tamara stared for a second and then ran off without answering. Miriam remained behind, watching as Tami disappeared into her house. Then she turned to go home, bewildered.

9 A Moment of Shock

IT WAS *SHABBOS* MORNING. MIRIAM'S HOUSE HUMMED. THE curtain over the *shul's* one small window had been thrown open, but even that barely helped. Thick, dark gray clouds covered the sky like a sad blanket, and a drizzle ran down the window pane like little tear stains.

But in the tiny *shul*, the light of *Shabbos* burned brightly. Miriam's father glowed, and the *shul* drew its radiance from him. When he was gloomy or worried, the *shul* darkened. When he was joyous, it was like the sun coming out after a rainfall, beaming glistening rainbows.

Today, Rabbi Levi was like a sunburst that no drizzle or

thunderclouds could dampen. He sang as he studied, and when he walked upstairs to bring down his cup of coffee, he practically danced.

"Great things are happening today," he declared to his wife as he poured steaming water from the samovar. "I feel it in my bones. I even found hints in today's *Parshah* . . ."

Needless to say, Luzer the Shmoozer was the first customer for the *minyan*. He smelled *Kiddush*. Miriam's mother had not only made a huge, bubbling *chulent*, but also hot *kugels*, potato and noodle, two long *kishkes* and various pickled salads.

There was no sponsor. Rabbi Levi himself set aside from the tight family funds to make a beautiful *Kiddush* in honor of Jill's Jewish naming. It was the return of a missing child to the Jewish fold. What could be more joyous?

Miriam stood on a chair and peered out the window. This way, she could see who was heading for their *minyan*, as she had a view almost to the end of the block.

It was unbelievable! Were all those people coming to the *shul*? It looked like the street leading to one of the great synagogues. Clumps of men and women, group behind group, headed in their direction. Miriam saw the neighbors peering out their front windows or standing at their doors, gazing at the unusual crowd. It made her a trifle uneasy. If any neighbor complained to City Hall, they would have trouble.

Not the faintest shadow of worry crossed Rabbi Levi's face. He greeted everyone broadly and warmly, even those who usually ignored his services. Today everything was forgiven and forgotten.

The service began promptly, and old Mr. Ingber droned through the opening prayers. He returned to his place, and

Rabbi Levi himself approached the *amud*. He pulled his *tallis* low over his head, raised his hands before him and sang in a full voice.

Miriam never heard her father sound so happy, so strong, so mighty, so warm, so confident, so carefree. The walls shook as he burst forth with the *davening*. The tightly packed congregation stood and sang along with the ancient melodies, caught in the fervor.

Higher, higher, higher! His voice rose, the words roared from his throat, from his stomach, his arms, his legs, from every muscle and fibre. Rabbi Levi's hands clasped the *tallis* closer and closer to his head, and his body swayed and shook back and forth, back and forth, like a tree in a hurricane.

The *tefillah* ended, followed by an instant silence. And then, even stronger, another explosion of melody! So sweet it was, a melody Miriam had never heard from her father before. She knew where it came from. It came from before, before the terrible time that her father kept sealed from her and her brothers, the time when her father did not have a long white beard but was a smooth faced boy, just like her silly brothers.

Everyone was caught in the song, everyone was in a trance of thoughts and melodies. Miriam wished she could put those few minutes away in a jar and save it for the rest of her life.

Just then, the upstairs door opened.

"There's not one more inch for another person," Mrs. Levi whispered to Miriam. People were squeezed next to each other like sardines.

A shadow at the top of the stairs hesitated, and slowly descended.

"It's Tamara," whispered Miriam excitedly. "She made it!"

Tamara paused on the stairs when she saw the huge throng. She looked bewildered and very shy. Miriam jumped up instantly and ran to her friend. She grabbed her hand and led her back to where she and her mother sat. Someone squeezed over a little, Miriam and her mother gave up part of their chairs, and there was room.

Tamara looked awful. Her dress was shabby, and despite the sunny weeks that had passed, she looked pale, like someone who hid in a closet all the time.

Miriam saw that her mother was surveying Tamara from head to toe. A frown formed on her face, but when Tami looked up, she hid it and smiled.

"Good *Shabbos*," she said and squeezed Tami's hands in her own.

Tami had grown shyer since last time. She didn't answer. She just watched as Miriam's father completed *Shacharis*. Before taking out the Torah from the *aron*, he turned to face the congregation.

Rabbi Levi's face was dazzling, crowned by the silver *atarah*. Though he did not usually address the congregation during the *davening*, he gazed about him intently and began to speak.

"*Rabbosai*! My friends! In a moment we will remove the Torah from the *Aron Hakodesh* and read this week's portion, *Bamidbar*. It describes forty years of wandering through the desert.

"What a terrible wilderness the ancient Israelites had to tramp through! Serpents and scorpions, searing heat, deadly enemies, Amalek!

"But the Jewish people knew where they were going.

They had a pillar of cloud by day and a pillar of fire by night to lead them. They had signs and banners, and the *Mishkan* in their midst. They were in a wilderness, but everyone knew where he belonged.

"Today we have another wilderness. No serpents or scorpions, plenty to eat and drink, but an even bleaker wilderness. We have forgotten from where we have come, and we do not know where we are going. We are wandering aimlessly, with no pillar, no cloud, no fire.

"But you stare at me and argue, 'Reb Mordechai, look at us. Here we are! We are in *shul*! We are wrapped in our *talleisim* of fine wool. We are celebrating *Shabbos.*'This is all true."

Rabbi Levi paused, looked momentarily at the ark, pulled at his *tallis* and continued.

"In a moment, we will take out our holy Torah. The scroll contains hundreds of thousands of letters. Each letter was meticulously inscribed by a pious scribe, with sacred intentions. Each time he formed the Holy Name, he shuddered with piety and awe.

"A great scroll. But what is a Torah if even one of the letters is missing? One letter! One tiny *yud*, one simple stroke of the quill. It is *pasul*, missing, unkosher. Why? It is so full of other sacred letters and words, what difference does one letter make? But that is the law. That has always been the law.

"The Jewish nation is a Torah also. Every Jewish soul is a letter in our Torah. We can wrap ourselves in a hundred *talleisim*, but if one Jew is missing, we are each incomplete."

Rabbi Levi paused, and Miriam held her breath. She knew that when her father hesitated in the middle of speaking, he was choked with feeling. But he would never show it. It was not his way. Whatever he felt was inside, deep.

Miriam's father caught himself and continued.

"Today, we will see another step towards our *Geulah*. A little girl who was far removed from our people is being given a Jewish name. It is Devorah, like the prophetess of old!

"But we are doing more than giving a name. We are giving her a letter of the Torah. Once it is hers, it can never be taken from her. Little Devorah, can you hear me back there?"

People strained to see Jill-Devorah, who hid for her life behind her mother.

"Today you are bound with our Torah!"

Rabbi Levi raised his fist and held it high. He was exuberant, his face shining with a heavenly light.

"*Freilich*, my friends!" he cried out. "For today we stand again at the foot of Mount Sinai! *Olelim veyonkim*, all the children. The Torah was given in the merit of the innocent children! Come, let us march with the Torah. Come, everyone, come!"

There was chaos as chairs were shuffled aside, and a happy pandemonium filled the room.

"Come on, Tami! Come to the front with me," Miriam urged her friend.

Tamara shook her head, a frightened look on her face.

"No, let me stay here, please," she pleaded. "I'm afraid."

Miriam lost her patience. Why did Tami always have to be different, always afraid?

"Come on," she urged. "Let's go watch!"

Tamara looked at Miriam with those pleading eyes.

"Please . . . my father. I'm afraid!"

"Miriam, leave Tamara alone," Mrs. Levi whispered. "She doesn't have to go if she doesn't want to."

Miriam pretended not to hear her mother. She knew Tami better than anyone. Tami had to be pulled into action. Miriam grabbed Tamara by the hand and yanked her from her seat.

"Your father is not here," Miriam reassured her. "It's safe. You're in my house. Come on, I'll be right next to you."

Tamara glanced around, looking for an escape. But Miriam would not let go. Tamara took a deep breath, held on to Miriam's hand so hard it hurt and followed her up to the *mechitzah*.

Rabbi Levi and his two elderly *gabboim* were squeezed into a tight circle by almost twenty little boys, who pressed forward to kiss the Torah. To make matters worse, Luzer pushed forward, brushed the Torah mantle with his dingy *tzitzis* and kissed them.

"What a tattered, old cover for the Torah," he clucked. "It's not nice to wrap a Torah in such an old thing."

Rabbi Levi raised the Torah high for everyone to see.

"Everyone, let us sing together!"

There was clapping and singing; the walls resounded. Miriam felt that a wall had come down just then, a wall that surrounded her father's heart. He seemed to forget himself and where he was, or the people, or his sadness, or her. His eyes were clamped shut in ecstasy, sweat rolling down his face and neck under the silver crested *tallis*. The room burned with feeling, and Rabbi Levi was the furnace. Miriam was so happy.

The excitement was at a pitch, the power of the holy moment strong. Even Tamara joined in the clapping as a joyous smile slowly spread across her face. She and Miriam watched in awe as Rabbi Levi began the short, dignified march with the Torah, his congregation swirling around him like a human sea.

The procession maneuvered through the front of the *shul* and had just turned down the short aisle near the women's section, when the room suddenly darkened.

Instinctively, Miriam looked up towards the small window. In the window was the face of Tamara's father! He was staring, glaring into the window, searching for his daughter.

Rabbi Levi halted the procession, shocked by the apparition in the window. Mr Kranz's gaunt face, his twisted pale lips, his long, sharp nose pressed against the window like in a bad dream.

He spotted Tami. She threw her hand to her mouth, and her eyes widened with fear. Rabbi Levi's *tallis* slipped off his head as he motioned towards Mr. Kranz and beckoned him to come in and join them. Rabbi Levi was shaken, but he tried to smile.

This infuriated Mr. Kranz even more. He glared back with hatred. Then he started rapping, rapping, rapping sharply, menacingly. Rap! Rap! Rap!

At first, there was silence.

"*Ah meshugenah!*" someone suddenly screamed.

"What does he want?" asked another.

Mr. Kranz gestured fiercely at Tamara, ordering her out. In response, Rabbi Levi pointed to the Torah cradled in his arms.

"*Luz ir bleibin,*" he called to Kranz. "Let her stay."

Rap, rap, rap!

"I have to go," Tami whimpered. "I have to go, Miriam."

"It's not fair!" Miriam shouted to Tami. "You're not doing anything wrong. It's *Shabbos.*"

"I have to go!" Tami screamed back hysterically.

She broke loose from Miriam's hand, forced her way through the crowd and flew up the stairs.

Rabbi Levi stood bewildered, then furious. He lifted his fist and waved it towards Mr. Kranz, who sprang towards Tamara as she approached.

"*Malach Hamovess!*" he screamed at Kranz. "Angel of Death!"

Kranz turned on his heel and headed back towards the window. He bent down with slow deliberation, lifted a stone the size of a baseball and with one quick move smashed the window pane. Everyone in the *shul* gasped.

Just then Tamara appeared behind him. He turned, and with a brusque gesture of his hand, he sent her home.

10 Nightmare City

THE BEAUTIFUL *SHABBOS* WAS RUINED. MIRIAM'S FATHER WAS so shaken by the window smashing that he collapsed into a chair after the Torah procession. Mrs. Levi ran to his side. Rabbi Levi put down his head on a table and covered himself with his *tallis*. He looked like he was going to pass out. Someone brought a glass of water, but the rabbi waved it away.

"I'm all right," he insisted.

He hoisted himself up, adjusted his *tallis* and proceeded to read the Torah. All the joy had vanished from his face. Devorah was named, there was the singing of *Siman Tov*, and the fancy *Kiddush* followed.

But the *Simchah* was ruined.

The *shul*, and soon the whole city, was buzzing with the story of the window smashing.

Miriam's parents finally squeezed the true story out of her. She told them about the first time she had gone to the Kranz house and been threatened, the secret meetings with Tamara, the tricks to get her to *shul* and the *Seder* incident. Her parents were amazed and infuriated.

For Miriam, it was nightmare city.

Miriam dreamed she was walking with her father, and they were suddenly being chased by a big black dog with yellow teeth and red eyes. Tati disappeared, and Miriam was on her own, running towards a narrow bridge over a deep ravine. The dog bolted after her, and the bridge got narrower and narrower. The dog jumped and . . .

Kranz was at the window! She saw him peering at her through the dark, even while she slept, helpless. How queer! It was impossible! How did he climb up the house wall to the second story window? And he wasn't even holding on. How silly.

He was waving his fist, glowering and gnashing his teeth. He took a rock and smash! The window broke, and he was climbing in. Mommy, Mommy!

Miriam woke up, shivering in her dark room. What was that noise outside? Now she was not dreaming. Maybe Mr. Kranz, that crazy, horrible Mr. Kranz, was outside. He only lived a few houses away. How could she be sure it wasn't him?

He could come into her room. It was possible. He could stalk around in the backyard, climb a tree and jump into her room.

What was that? Definitely a sound in the backyard. Was it a cat, a squirrel? Maybe it was Kranz, ugly, bony Mr. Kranz, coming after her in revenge. After all, it was she who had taught Tami to read Hebrew; it was she who invited Tami to *shul*.

Miriam was frightened. She couldn't fall back asleep. She could go to her parents, but they were fast asleep. No, she mustn't wake them. She threw off her cover and climbed onto the floor.

What time was it anyway? Two thirty in the morning. She must be the only one awake in the whole city. She opened her curtain slightly and peered out the window. A silver moon floated over Bathurst Street, and the leaves of the backyard trees glowed eerily. Kranz could be anywhere out there, hiding among the branches or in the back shed. There was the sound of a siren, then silence.

There was only one thing to do. She hated it, but one does what one has to do. She gathered her dignity and marched into Izzy's and Dizzy's room.

Yech!

It was a small room across from hers, but with a big bunk-bed. The upper bunk was empty. All day long, Izzy and Dizzy fought about everything, beat each other, called each other names, threatened mercilessly. Every night, they squeezed next to each other, their heads buried in two pillows, the cover mushed up between them. They were afraid of the dark.

The room looked like a war zone. Every single drawer was sticking out. There were shirts all over the floor, underwear on the ceiling light, a *Shabbos* jacket hanging on the door-knob, two bats, a baseball glove and a basketball on the floor and books flying everywhere. You had to *bentch Gomel* whenever you left the room safely.

Miriam climbed to the top bed, covered herself and float-ed peacefully off to sleep. She knew that if Kranz ever broke into *this* room, he would fall over something before he could do anything!

11   A Difficult Decision

SOMETHING WAS NOT RIGHT. THE STREET HAD CHANGED. Miriam could smell it. Her father had bought their house four years before his heart attack and had opened his *shul* in the basement. It was his whole life now. The *shul* was not illegal, but it wasn't official either. If no one complained, there was no problem. But if even one neighbor called City Hall, a by-law officer could come and make her father close the *shul*. That would break his heart.

So far, no one complained. The Levis were blessed with wonderful neighbors. Mr. Johnson, a retired butcher, lived on one side. A quiet family, shy but very kind, lived on the other. Across the street was an elderly couple who always waved *"Good Shabbos"* to them. Down the street lived Italian and Greek families who were always very respectful.

Since the *Shabbos* of the window smashing and the great horde of people who attended the service, the street turned chilly. People averted their eyes, and the greetings were quick and minimal.

"I knew I shouldn't have let Tati invite so many people that *Shabbos*," Miriam's mother confided to her as they prepared a small *Kiddush* the following week. "It scared everyone on the block. And then that horrible man, that Kranz!"

A shiver ran down Miriam's spine at the mention of his name.

It was a glorious time of the year in Toronto. Ontario Place had opened up. Canada's Wonderland was packed with school buses. White sailboats filled the aqua-green waters of Lake Ontario, which sparkled in the June sunshine. Maple, oak and willow trees luxuriated in the lush Ontario soil, crowning the streets with rich green foliage. Down the block, carefree little children played in the cul-de-sac, peddling their tricycles and dodging skateboards. School finally ended.

Toronto was warm, warm, warm. Finally!

But Miriam was not happy. Tamara was not to be seen . . . ever! Miriam had crazy thoughts that she was locked up in her room, maybe even . . . killed? During the school year, Miriam glimpsed Tami occasionally at least, from a distance. But now! It bothered her, it bothered her to her very toes, to her very stomach, to her very roots.

"Tati," she finally asked one day, "we must do something to find Tami. What should we do?"

Rabbi Levi, who was studying on the back deck, put down his *sefer* and looked apologetic.

"I don't know," he said. "We must be careful to make sure there is no trouble. We have a great problem, *shainkeit*. A great problem."

"Problem?" asked Miriam. "What problem?"

Rabbi Levi sighed and tugged at his beard.

"We must be very discreet," he explained. "Mr. Johnson next door is our friend. He would never cause trouble. But he tells me some of the neighbors are thinking of complaining about the *shul*. They claim we are getting bigger, which is true, and causing a disturbance. We must be very quiet, very quiet."

"But how can we leave Tamara alone?" Miriam persisted.

Rabbi Levi shook his head sadly.

"You are right," he said. "But if her father were a normal person, someone reasonable, we could discuss it with him. But you saw how he acted, Miriam. He is a lunatic! I pity him, Miriam, and I pity Tamara, but I'm also afraid of what he might do. He could destroy everything we've built, end all the good work I am trying to do."

"But isn't there something we could do?" pressed Miriam. "Couldn't we call the government, the police, someone?"

"*Chas veshalom*," Miriam's father answered adamantly. "Call the police on a fellow Jew? *Chas veshalom*. Whatever we do must be within our own community, among ourselves. Call the government? Call strangers?"

He lifted up his *sefer*, appalled at Miriam's suggestion. The discussion was over. Miriam saw that her father was deeply upset, caught in a terrible dilemma. There was nothing he could do.

Miriam accepted her father's answer for a day or two. He

had spoken. There was nothing to do.

But like something you eat that sits in your stomach and grows more and more uncomfortable, his answer could not be digested. Miriam felt sick inside, thinking about Tamara.

Poor Tami.

But her father had spoken.

But Tami was her friend.

But *kibbud av v'em*, honoring a father and mother, was one of the most sacred *mitzvos* in the Torah.

It was the last week in June, the heart of the beautiful summer. Tamara kept appearing in Miriam's dreams, begging and pleading with her to come to her rescue. Those sad eyes. Miriam imagined they were peering at her by day and in her sleep.

One sunny, lazy *Shabbos* afternoon, Miriam found time to think. The Levis lived a few blocks south of Earl Bales Park, a rambling wooded space, with many secret paths, dark woods and a secret river, hidden deep in a valley. The park was full of *frum* families, swinging their children. Old people sunned themselves on the benches.

Miriam greeted a few children she knew but then headed around the clubhouse to the road that fell steeply to the riverbank. She wanted to be alone, very much alone with the woods and with Hashem.

She was nervous. A young girl, she knew, should not be in this secluded spot alone. Hashem should forgive her. But this was her thinking place, her private place under a tall, twisted pine.

Everything was so bad. Tami was gone, a prisoner. Just two houses away, but she might as well be in Siberia. Tati was in trouble because of his *shul*. Her parents were frightened, too. She could feel it. Even her mother, who was usually calm, had begun to look frightened. If the *shul* closed, their whole life would be destroyed and maybe even her father's health.

That crazy Kranz! Why did he have to live here? Why did she knock on their door? Her parents had been right. Keep away!

Rabbi Levi was from Europe. He had lived through the Holocaust, and Canada was a foreign country. Everything was strange to him, everything was frightening. In his life, government meant police, and police meant trouble. That's all they needed now, trouble with the crazy man down the block.

She must just let it go. There was no room for trouble.

But what about Tamara?

Who would save Tamara?

Who would help her escape?

Who would teach her Yiddishkeit?

Who would defend Tamara?

Her parents had warned her. But it was up to Miriam and no one else. She stood up and blew her curl upward furiously. She would have to do it now, right now, right on *Shabbos*, before she lost her nerve.

The Kranz house was hidden behind two thick evergreens, so that the entrance was barely visible from the street. Miriam trembled. She was terrified. Before she lost her nerve, she quickly climbed the stairs, took a deep breath and knocked on the door carefully.

There was no response. Instinctively, she stepped back from the door and tried to peer into the front window. But the window was covered by a huge white shade. Not even a corner was exposed.

Miriam knocked again, harder. She waited tensely. Out on

the street were the sounds of the neighborhood, cars passing, children on skates, a radio playing in someone's backyard. But this porch, hidden behind dark trees, was a silent world unto itself. Miriam put her ear to the door. Was that a sound of footsteps inside? She couldn't press too hard, because the paint was peeling on the door, scratching her. Was that a sound or not? She couldn't tell.

Perhaps she should walk around to the side door and try there. But that meant getting deep into Kranz property. She was afraid.

Finally, she stood up straight and smoothed her skirt. She was proud. She had tried. She had gone right up to the Kranz door and knocked, once, twice. She had fulfilled the *mitzvah* of loving one's neighbor. She was morally free to leave, and she turned and walked down the stairs, breathing more easily. Each step brought her closer to safety.

Miriam Levi, you are full of baloney! You are fooling yourself, not Hashem. You knocked like a mouse. You knocked low enough that no one could hear you. Tamara is somewhere inside that creepy house, and you failed her. You are a coward.

In a fury, she blew at her curl, turned around and flew up the stairs. She pounded like an army officer. Bang, bang, bang! Let the whole door shatter!

Suddenly, the door opened, and Mr. Kranz towered over her. His face was an angry stone. He didn't say anything, just glared at her.

"G-good *Shabbos*," Miriam blurted out, trying to control her fright. "I came to play with Tamara. Is she home?"

He just stared at her like an angry dog. Miriam had a chance to see him clearly in the afternoon sunlight. He was so very pale, with parchment-like skin. He was older than

Miriam had thought, and shorter. She repeated her request.

"It's so nice outside," she said. "I thought Tamara might like to spend *Shabbos* with me. Is she home?"

He began closing the door in her face.

"She's not here," he muttered.

"Where is she?" Miriam pressed desperately. "Maybe I can find her."

He glowered at her even harder.

"I said I don't know where she is. Goodbye." He moved to shut the door in her face.

"Miriam!"

Miriam looked inside the house. It was Tamara! She was standing in the dark dining room, far back. The room was so dim she could hardly see her.

"Miriam, *Good Shabbos!*"

Miriam scowled at Kranz. Anger overcame fear.

"You lied," she accused him. "Tami *is* home. Tami, I came for you!"

But Tamara suddenly lost her tongue. She stood rooted to the spot, almost as though she were chained to it.

"Goodbye! Goodbye!" Mr. Kranz shouted at Miriam.

Miriam lost her temper.

"Why can't I come in?" she demanded. "Why can't Tamara come out to play with me? What is wrong? What are you doing to her?"

The reaction was swift. Kranz's face twisted with fury, and the door exploded open. He was holding something, a glass bird, with a sharp ugly beak. He raised it over Miriam's head.

"Get out of here, you!" he screamed. "Get out of here before I crack this over your head!"

He rushed at Miriam. She flew down the steps in complete panic, almost falling on her face. He ran after her like a wild dog, the bird clenched in his bony fingers.

She ran past the trees, onto the street. She ran towards her house and safety. In front of her own house, she turned. Kranz had stopped at the edge of his front yard, his little territory.

"I'll get you, you little busybody," he shouted after her. "I'll get you good, all of you!"

12 Izzy and Dizzy

MIRIAM RAN INTO HER HOUSE IN TERROR. SHE QUICKLY climbed the stairs, ran into her room and shut the door firmly behind her. Should she put something to block the door? There was no lock. Had Kranz followed her? She carefully lifted the side of her shade and peered out. Two boys walked past, laughing about something. There was a drone of a plane banking overhead. Across the street, the sound of a lawn mower hummed.

Everything seemed so normal.

Shaking, she burst into quiet tears. Her parents must not hear her. She buried her face in the pillow. The afternoon sunlight bathed the room in a balmy glow, like a warm bath. She cried and cried until she fell asleep.

She dreamed and saw Mr. Kranz's ugly, ugly face staring at her, gnashing his teeth.

She dreamed and saw Tamara's face staring at her, angry!

She dreamed and the whole world watched her with enormous angry eyes—her father, her mother, Mrs. Blum her *dikduk* teacher, the old men of the *shul*, angry, angry, at wicked Miriam!

"What have you done?" she whimpered to herself, half asleep, half awake.

The noise of Izzy and Dizzy playing in the backyard with some friends woke her up. She looked at the clock. It was late, after seven. She climbed out of bed and checked herself in the bathroom mirror. Her face looked ghastly; eyes red, cheeks dark with tear stains.

That's all she needed now! Her parents would take one look and demand to know what happened. If they knew what she had done, there would be one grand fuss.

Why couldn't she have minded her own business? She had made things worse for everyone—for herself, for her parents and, above all, for Tamara.

Poor Tami. What was happening to her now?

Miriam washed her face in cold water. The water felt good. She tested her face, flickered her eyes cheerily and practiced smiling.

Smile, smile, she reminded herself. Maybe she should slip over to a friend's house before her parents saw her. No, she had to help set *Shalosh Seudos*.

She opened the door and walked carefully downstairs. She could hear her father teaching the weekly *Pirkei Avos* to his students. Her mother was in the kitchen, fishing out pieces of marinated herring for the meal.

"Can I help, Mom?" Miriam asked brightly.

"Yes," said her mother, not bothering to look up. "Please get two onions from the bottom drawer."

Miriam quickly brought out two onions and laid them on the table in front of her mother.

Her mother looked up and Miriam gave her a bright smile, fluttering her eyelids.

Mrs. Levi put down the fork quickly and stared piercingly at her daughter.

"Miriam, what's the matter?"

"Ma-matter?" answered Miriam brightly. "Nothing is the matter."

"Miriam, you are lying. And on *Shabbos*, too. What is the matter?"

Miriam hugged her mother very hard, hiding her face.

"No, Mommy. Everything is fine. I'm just tired."

There was an uneasy quiet for a moment, and Miriam's mother reached for the herring jar again.

"Okay, darling, if you say so."

She didn't ask any further questions. She knew something was the matter, and Miriam knew that she knew. But Leah Levi also knew when to step back, and Miriam loved her mother dearly for it. She let Miriam be her own person.

Miriam did not have much time to dwell on her problems after *Shabbos*. The Levi household was frantic that night, well past midnight. Izzy and Dizzy were going to camp on Sunday morning, and they had everyone climbing the walls.

"Where are my other socks?"

"Where's my blue shirt?"

"My *tzitzis* need to be washed."

"I can't find my small suitcase!"

"You stole my glove!"

If they hadn't been Miriam's own brothers, she might even have enjoyed them. They were so funny together, always full of life, telling riddles, making up plays, memorizing *Mishnayos*, wrestling, slugging each other and then curling up together each night like two puppies.

Leah worked way past midnight getting their stuff ready, while Rabbi Levi escaped to the *shul* downstairs. To make matters more frantic, a boys' choir record blasted on the stereo, and Luzer the Shmoozer parked himself in the middle of the living room, since he was going with the boys on the bus the next morning.

But for Miriam, all the tumult was a blessing. Everything was so lively and cheerful, so normally hectic, so protected by her parents, that she felt safe and far removed from the terrible scene earlier in the day. She even wondered if it had really happened or if she had dreamed it during her *Shabbos* afternoon nap.

In the middle of all the frenzy, Luzer begged for a cup of coffee, and Miriam quickly prepared it for him. She handed it to him and he balanced it carefully on his enormous knee. And then, just before he lifted it to make a *berachah*, he said something that genuinely startled Miriam and her mother.

"You know," he said benignly, "I love your family. I really do. They are so kind to me. You have all been so nice to me. Someday I'll pay you back, and the Rebbe, too. You'll see."

He lifted the coffee, a tranquil, faraway look in his eyes. Coming from Luzer, who hardly ever opened his mouth except to ask for food, it was surprising.

"Thank you, Luzer," Leah answered. "That's very sweet."

Eventually, the packing was finished. Luzer went home, and peace descended.

But just for a few hours. Sunday morning was absolute bedlam. Last minute laundry was gathered, and Izzy and Dizzy were frantic with excitement. Luzer arrived at the house with a huge satchel that looked like it contained an atomic bomb. Mrs. Levi drove their old station wagon, with the children, Rabbi Levi, the extra luggage and Luzer, who squeezed himself into the back seat. He was the last one to leave the house, and his atomic bomb satchel almost hit everyone as he climbed in. He had *schnorred* himself a ride on the camp bus that was going halfway to Montreal.

Funny, thought Miriam. After the nice words he said last night, I'm going to miss him.

Piles of luggage, duffel bags, tennis rackets and baseball bats surrounded the three buses at the school parking lot. Everything was crammed into the storage compartments, and after being *shlepped* back for one more good-bye kiss from their parents, the children boarded the buses. Miriam never even got a chance to say good-bye, but she did wave.

They scrambled up the steps, Izzy, Dizzy and Luzer, hardly able to get through the bus doors. Leah Levi took a deep breath of relief.

"*Baruch Hashem*," sighed Rabbi Levi. "It is we who are on vacation, not they."

And they headed back to the peace and quiet of their home.

13 **An Act of Revenge**

MIRIAM WOKE UP ON MONDAY MORNING, AND IMMEDIATELY knew something was very wrong. How did she know right away? she later asked herself. It was very still without Izzy or Dizzy, but that was not unusual. No, it was the sound of whispering, coming through the floor from below.

Her father and mother were downstairs in the kitchen, talking in strange, hushed tones. Had someone died? Miriam quickly washed her hands, threw on her robe and padded downstairs in her bare feet.

Her father was sitting at the breakfast table, his head buried in his hands. Her mother stood over him, a cup of coffee in her hands, not moving. Was he sick? Miriam ran to him, to hug him.

"Leave Tati alone," Leah screamed at her. It was a shriek Miriam had never heard before from her mother.

"What is it?" Miriam demanded, yelling back. "Is Tati sick? Tell me, Tati, are you all right?"

Rabbi Levi lifted his large head, like a risen lion, and stared at his daughter silently. His beard seemed to have grown whiter overnight, or was it her imagination?

Miriam looked to him, to her mother. Why didn't they say anything, tell her?

"What is it?" she persisted. "What happened?"

"Come, I will show you, *shainkeit*," said Rabbi Levi.

He lifted his great frame, and with Miriam and Leah following, descended to the *shul*. He walked over to the *Aron Hakodesh*, kissed the *parochess* and pulled it aside. He swung open the doors.

The precious family heirloom, the Romanian Torah, was gone!

Miriam looked up at her father, bewildered.

"Someone has stolen our Torah," she whispered.

It was then that it all came tumbling down on Miriam. What she had hidden even from her dreams, what she had not wanted to think about. It flew at her like a night demon, the horror next door.

She knew where the Torah had gone. The monster had kept his word, found his revenge. He did it! Kranz had taken their Torah.

Rabbi Levi took one last long look at the empty spot, sighed and closed the doors. He cleared his throat and sniffled deeply. Miriam knew what that sniffle and grunt meant. Her father was trying to fight back his tears, angry at himself for being weak. Inside, he was crying.

There was a momentary silence.

"Let's go back upstairs," Leah suggested. "There's no reason to stay down here."

They marched upstairs, and no one spoke. It was the longest walk Miriam had ever taken, for in those few seconds she had to decide.

Should she tell them who had taken the Torah? Should she confess that it was all her fault, that she had disobeyed them and gone again to the Kranz house? If she told them, they would call the police, or her father would immediately run to the Kranz house and maybe have a heart attack, maybe even . . .

She had mixed into what was not her business. She had not listened. If she told them everything, her parents would hate her. They'd be furious at her and never love her the same way again, never trust her.

Should she tell?

No. It was her problem, her problem alone. She had caused the Torah to be taken, and she must get it back herself, somehow. She blew at her curl and kept her mouth shut.

They reached the kitchen, and Leah again handed the coffee cup to her husband.

"Call the police, Mordechai," she urged. "There is no other choice now."

He shook his head firmly.

"No," he said.

"Why not?" she demanded impatiently.

He paused, measuring his words.

"There is something happening here," he replied in a low voice, "something I don't understand."

Just for an instant, his gaze ran over the room. Miriam looked away. Was he staring at her? Miriam walked to the large picture window and watched the birds flit among the little green apples.

"Who took the Torah?" he continued. "And why was it taken? Why now, just now? Who would want a stolen Torah? No, there is something more."

He took a sip of the coffee, calmly, as though this were just another Monday. He was like a lion, crouching, waiting, watching.

"What is it, Mordechai?" his wife pressed him. "What are you saying? What are you thinking?"

"There is a story hidden here," he mused. "Something we don't know."

Again, his great eyes fixed on Miriam. Why did he have to look at her like that?

"Someone took the Torah," he continued. "Why didn't we hear him come in? The house was locked, and nothing was broken. No, there is a test here, a heavenly plan I don't understand."

"You are just fooling yourself," Leah interrupted. "The whole city knew what a valuable scroll you had. Someone simply broke into the house and stole the Torah. There is always a market for a Torah in New York, or somewhere else. There are ugly people who will steal anything, trade in anything, even stolen *Sifrei Torah*." Her voice rose. "Call the police, that is what you must do! All this philosophy is simply because you are afraid to call the police."

Rabbi Levi looked up at his wife, like a child addressing his mother.

"You are right, Leah, I am afraid," he said. "Don't think calling the police is such a holiday. There will be questions about everything and about everyone who ever walked into this house. The whole city will be talking about us. Everything will be investigated."

"Let them investigate," Leah urged. "We have nothing to hide and neither does anyone who *davens* here."

Rabbi Levi's eyebrows rose upward, and a faint smile flickered across his lips. Everyone has secrets, a public face and a private face. Who knows what they will uncover?

Then he did a strange thing. He put down his cup, turned to Miriam and gave her a little smile. Miriam tried to smile back, but inside she shook.

"So that's it, then," Leah threw up her hands. "That's your plan. Say goodbye to the precious Torah that your family prized for two hundred years. What will you do now?"

"The Torah will not run away. King Solomon said there is a time for everything, even discovery. We will wait." He turned to Miriam. "What do you think, *shainkeit*? Shall we wait for the truth?"

Miriam gulped. She could hardly speak.

14 The Invisible Cord

MIRIAM RAN UP TO HER ROOM AND LOCKED THE DOOR. SHE had a baby sitting job in the afternoon, but now she had to think.

In her younger days, like the previous month, Miriam would have burst out crying or covered her head with a pillow and dreamed black dreams. But now her father's trusting face burned into her, and her mother's frustration moved her; she knew it was a time not for tears but for action.

She was mad. Her father and mother were both good people. They never hurt anyone on purpose. They opened their doors to everyone. They struggled from day to day. They were survivors. And one mean, insane person, crazy Mr. Kranz had ruined their lives. He took the only thing, except their children, that meant anything to them.

She was not going to stand for it. This is Canada. This is a country with laws. She would fight back. Alone, if necessary.

She had to reach Tamara somehow. But how? Tami had disappeared. She was a prisoner in her own home, locked in by fear.

The next days were strained and strange. Time seemed to have stopped. There was a weird quiet with Izzy and Dizzy away. Thank Heaven, Luzer was also gone!

Miriam's father buried himself in his Talmud, her mother went about her business. There was little conversation, but Miriam had the eerie feeling that her parents were constantly watching her, studying her.

What should she do? She was in great trouble.

Her mother, her father, her teachers, her holy books, had taught her what to do under the circumstances. Miriam *davened* her heart out each morning. She usually woke up late, past eight, after her father had finished *Shacharis* and gone on his hospital visits. She had the little basement *shul* all to herself.

She usually left the light off, and the room was cool and dark. Only one little bulb twinkled like a little gold flame above the *Aron Hakodesh*. Across the room, one lone sunbeam peered through the small front window.

She did not use her regular *siddur*. There was a thick *siddur* almost a hundred years old, left by her mother's grandfather. It was rebound with thick black covers and had not only the regular *tefillos* but all sorts of holy writings and mystical names. Her mother told her it was very powerful and mysterious and had been used by a certain *tzaddik*.

She opened the tightly bound pages and poured her heart out. The words came out of her slowly, painfully. She embroidered the ancient, browning letters with her own tears.

"Oh, Hashem, it was all my fault! We must get back that Torah. And quickly! What will happen to my poor father if he doesn't find the Torah soon? He will get terribly sick.

"And what about Tamara? I must reach her somehow. How can I do it without You? Please, let the *kedushah* of this *siddur* carry my words to You."

She finished *davening* and returned the precious *siddur* to its place, high up. She didn't want her parents to discover that she had used it. They might be angry.

Miriam was about to go up to breakfast, when she paused and sat down in her regular seat in the woman's section. She wasn't hungry anyway. She rested her head in her hands, just like her father sometimes did when he was deep in thought. She closed her eyes and concentrated hard, hard, hard. All thoughts flew away, except for one.

Tamara!

"Tami, Tami," she whispered in her head. "Tami, my secret sister, can you hear me? We are attached by an invisible cord, aren't we? I need to talk to you right away, do you hear? I am in big trouble, and so are you. Your father has our Torah, and it's because of you and me. Tami, Tami, I need you!"

Over and over she sent the message. She sent it in her imagination through the window, down the street, over the bushes, the pine trees, through Tami's upstairs window, into her room, into her head.

Feeling better, she went upstairs to breakfast. It was

Friday but strangely quiet. Half the city was away. Thank goodness for her mother's-helper job. Today, Sarah Holz planned a visit to Center Island with her children, and Miriam was to go along and help.

Miriam loved Sarah Holz and dreamed of being just like her when she grew up. Sarah was young, pretty, wore beautiful but not flashy clothing, no polyester, a *shaitel* that looked like natural hair and always smiled and laughed. She was always happy and confident. Everything was fun for her. She never gossiped; she was too happy. If one of her children squashed his ice cream on his shirt, she never lost her temper but laughed instead. In Clanton Park, she swung on the swings like one of the children.

It was a beautiful July day, warm but not hot, and the lake breezes cooled them as they stood on the deck of the ferry. Toronto's skyline, with the CN Tower, skyscrapers and harbor front landings, look like a toy city.

Miriam forgot herself on Center Island and its rides. There was no time to worry or think about anything. She pushed the stroller over grassy hills and down lanes. There was no budget and no limit for the children. They did all the rides, the model train, the pony trail, even the scary cable cars. Her skin darkened in the bright sunshine. The clouds passed across the clear blue sky like little fluffy pillows.

The stolen Torah and all the problems at home seemed a thousand miles away. She wanted to confide in Sarah about the missing Torah and about Tamara, but her parents had strictly forbidden her to discuss the Torah with anyone. They didn't want the whole city talking.

It was past six when they rode the ferry back to the city. Seagulls dived overhead, sailboats played tag with the ferry, and the skyline of Toronto towered over them in all its majesty. It was a beautiful sight.

When Miriam came home, her mother was waiting for her, practically at the front door.

"Miriam, someone left an envelope for you," she said.

Miriam took the envelope. There was no return address, just her name. But Miriam knew who had written it. The small, tight print was instantly recognizable. It was from Tamara.

Mrs. Levi knew enough not to ask questions. Miriam took the envelope and ran up to the privacy of her own room. She locked the door behind her.

The envelope was small and dingy, as though it had been lying around in some drawer for a long time. Carefully, Miriam opened the envelope down the side and found a small piece of paper folded over twice. Miriam laid it out on her desk.

Dear Miriam,

I think about you all the time. I really mean it. I miss you very much. Do you miss me?

Please, I must see you. My father is acting stranger and stranger. I can meet you Sunday at 1:30 in the afternoon at the bottom of the ravine. Please, please be there. Okay?

I love you.

Tamara

P.S. Please, please be there!

Miriam reread the note a few times, trying to understand each word. Her father was acting stranger and stranger. What did that mean? Did he feel guilty because of the Torah? Had he harmed it?

And why had she written the note just today? Had the sacred *siddur* helped? Had she been able to send her thoughts out, like a radio message? Did she have special powers?

Her mother was calling her from downstairs. There was no time now to figure out anything. Miriam was just filled with happiness. Hashem had helped! She hid the letter deep under her mattress and ran downstairs to her mother.

15 *Kiddush Levanah*

IT WAS A QUIET, QUIET *SHABBOS*, LIKE THE QUIET BEFORE A storm. Izzy, Dizzy, Luzer and many of the congregation were away. There was barely a *minyan*.

If anyone noticed the missing Torah, nothing was said about it. There was a second Torah which had come from a downtown *shul* which had closed, and it was used for the reading.

Miriam watched her father closely. How much she loved him. He was holding himself in. He was so calm. Too calm. They read the portion of *Chukas*, in which Moshe Rabbeinu was punished for losing his self-control when in his anger, he struck the rock. Was that why her father was trying especially hard to be so cool, so self-reserved?

Her father was always moody like the sky, sunlight and storms, thunder and lightning, and warm loving rains. Now he was a still, heavy sky. Quiet. Waiting.

On *Motzoai Shabbos*, the family was usually summoned down to the *shul* to hear *Havdalah*. But this week was the beginning of the lunar month.

"*Rabbosai*!" Rabbi Levi announced. "Please take your *siddurim*. We will go out to the front of the house for *Kiddush Levanah*."

Her father and the men marched outside and made a half circle on the lawn. They read by the light of the street lamp, oblivious to the cars passing by.

It started to cloud up, but high above, a half moon could be seen sailing across the gaps in the clouds, like a sailing ship bent on a journey.

Rabbi Levi looked at the moon for a moment, grunted with satisfaction and reminded his congregants not to gaze at the moon as they recite the *berachah*, for it might appear that they were praying to the moon.

They all struggled to find the right page in the dim light. Suddenly, the rabbi lowered his *siddur* and faced his little congregation.

"My friends, when a Jew is in great trouble, the only way to overcome it is with joy. Tonight is such a night, the beginning of a new week. It is not enough to race through the words. Come, read with me!"

He lifted up the *siddur*, looked again at the moon and recited each word aloud, as though reading it for the first time. The men mumbled the words along with their rabbi. He paused.

"No, no!" he shouted impatiently. "Not so quiet. Not so cold. With *hislahavus*! With feeling!"

"But what about the neighbors?" worried Yitzchak, Rabbi Levi's loyal *gabbai*. "If we're too loud, they will complain. There might be trouble."

"We mustn't be afraid," Rabbi Levi responded sharply. "For too long we have been afraid. *I* have been afraid. We have been like mice hiding in a cellar. What do we have to be ashamed about? We have Torah. We have *mitzvos*. We have a *Ribono Shel Olam*. We must have *bitachon*. Come, Reb Yitzchak! With a *bren*, with fire!"

The men raised their voices so loud that Miriam and her mother could hear them inside.

"We will sing like when I was a child," Rabbi Levi announced. "Come, let's take each other's hands."

Self-consciously, the old men held hands and formed a small circle around Rabbi Levi.

"*Dovid Melech Yisrael, chai vikayom . . .*" he began a melody.

In a hoarse blend of wizened voices, the *minyan* sang and danced with their rabbi. They began slowly and awkwardly. No one ever danced *Chassid* style in the little *shul*. There was no room, and it was not Rabbi Levi's usual way.

But now, he broke loose of some inner chains. He was a lion, roaring. He led the circle and dragged the poor old men with him. They forgot themselves, feet flying, voices ringing out. They danced and danced, a bonfire of souls.

Cars slowed to stare, neighbors stood on their porches and watched the strange scene. Passing teenagers hooted in derision. Miriam's father heard nothing. His long black coat flew higher and back, his legs twirled and jigged, sweat poured down his great forehead.

Finally, the circle slowed down, exhausted and joyous. Rabbi Levi stuck out his hand to each man.

"*Shalom aleichem!*"

"*Aleichem shalom!*" answered Reb Yitzchak.

"*Shalom aleichem!*"

"*Aleichem shalom!*" answered Ingber.

"*Shalom aleichem!*"

"*Aleichem shalom!*"

The men shook hands, patted each other on the back and concluded the service.

"*Ah gut vuch! Ah gutten chodesh!*" Rabbi Levi blessed them.

The *minyan* straggled homeward.

Rabbi Levi returned to the *shul*, and Miriam joined him for *Havdalah*. She held the tapered beeswax candle while her father held the wine and the spices carrying the scent of Paradise. The room lights were shut, and the *Havdalah* light cast giant shadows on the ceiling. It was a precious time.

"Mordechai, what came over you?" Leah Levi asked.

Rabbi Levi looked at her steadily.

"This afternoon, after the *chulent*, I lay down and napped. I dreamed I saw our missing Torah. It was bright and joyous and glowing. No harm had come to it. A wave of joy and pleasure passed over me, and then I awoke.

"But that glow never left me. I feel the Torah itself sending a message to me. I feel it so close. I feel . . . I feel everything will be good. I feel . . ."

He stopped, as Leah and Miriam stared at him in dismay. Rabbi Levi, the great lion, was crying like a child.

16 The Hidden Ravine

THERE WAS A DEEP RAVINE AT THE END OF MIRIAM'S STREET where she was forbidden to go alone. It led down from the street, sloping steeply through a heavy forest of maple, oak and sycamore trees. It ended at the edge of a narrow creek that flowed through a dark tunnel into the Don River. It was a beautiful, hidden forest, winding and surprising, like a picture postcard. You would never know you were just two blocks from Bathurst Street.

Miriam knew it was not safe for her to go there alone. Dogs were let loose by their owners to run there, and you never knew who was hiding behind the bushes.

But, technically, she was not all by herself if she met Tamara there, was she? She had an answer if her parents found out.

Secondly, did she have a choice?

It was a beautiful Sunday afternoon in July, and she had no trouble getting away. She told her mother she was going out to play with friends. That was true. Her mother barely paid attention, nodded and let her go.

But Miriam did not take chances. She walked to Bathurst, double-checked that no one was watching her from her house, ran around Lyone Gate and doubled back to the ravine.

She entered warily, keeping her eye open for anything unusual. It was exciting, this mission. The road descended rapidly, turning gracefully like a lovely country lane, with walls and walls of trees.

Where was Tamara? She didn't say where to meet. Someone was walking up around the bend. It was an old couple. They nodded pleasantly, whispered something, and then she was alone again.

She was halfway down now. There were two side roads on the left following streams that led back up the hills to Earl Bales Park. She reached the end of the forest, and it opened to a dusty field. On the left was a tall link fence, the edge of the park.

Miriam looked around. Tamara was nowhere to be seen. In the far distance, there was a sound of barking. Miriam was afraid. Were dogs coming down? She checked her watch. One thirty-eight, just the time Tamara had said.

A battered old car roared down the road into the field. The people inside saw her, made a U-turn and left as quickly as they had come.

Miriam was all alone and frightened. Should she call out loud? What was there to lose?

"Tamara!" she shouted, letting her voice stretch up to the treetops. "Tamara!"

Silence, complete silence. Miriam waited. One forty. One forty-five. Five more minutes, she told herself. Five more minutes, and then she must go.

A large dark cloud crept across the face of the sun, casting a sad shadow. There was a twinge of cool wind. The cloud rolled away, and again the field was bathed in warm sunshine.

Miriam sighed. It was almost two o'clock. Slowly, she headed back up the ravine. She had not been down this way for a while, and she had forgotten how utterly private and beautiful and unspoiled it was. She walked up slowly, counting the wild flowers that grew along the road.

"Miriam . . ."

Miriam froze. It was Tamara, whispering to her from somewhere.

"Miriam!"

Miriam answered in an equally low voice.

"Tami, I hear you, but I can't see you."

"Here I am."

Miriam turned around. Tamara stood behind her. She had materialized mysteriously like a forest sprite.

Miriam ran down to Tamara and hugged her. It was like hugging a bag of bones. In the month they had been separated, Tamara had grown taller and skinnier, like an unkept weed. She wore an ugly grey skirt and a yellow blouse.

"I missed you," Tamara whispered.

"I missed you, too," Miriam answered. "I was really worried about you. I even sent you a *neshamah* message, a mind message. Did you get it?"

"I think so. I kept on talking to you in my head also."

"When did you get the note to me?"

"About two o'clock. My father sent me to get milk. I had to see you, so I took a chance. You know. I used the old trick. I came around the block and around the other way."

"You look so pale," Miriam blurted out.

Tamara didn't answer, and for a second her dark, black eyes blanked out with a distracted look.

"Miriam, I had to see you. I'm really afraid."

Miriam stepped closer and took her hand.

"Afraid? Afraid of what? Don't be afraid. I'm with you now. I'll help you. Let's walk."

She guided her up the road. Tamara held back.

"No, someone will see us together."

"So let them see us," Miriam answered impatiently. "Let the whole world see us. You're not doing anything wrong."

"But my father may see us."

"Tami," Miriam said in hushed, calm tones. "You have to take a stand. You can't be a weakling. You can't always be afraid of your father. He doesn't own you. Come!"

She pulled Tamara's hand and led her upwards. Tamara walked slowly, reluctantly. But she followed, at first between the trees, then more openly. Miriam knew she had won the first round.

Just as they were about to turn the last bend onto the street, Miriam stopped and began working on her problem. She turned to face Tamara.

"Why haven't I seen you all these weeks? What has been happening?"

Tamara tried to talk.

"My father . . ."

Then she choked and became still. Tamara seemed para-lyzed, unable to open her mouth to expel the words. Miriam found herself imitating her own mother, balancing just the right tones of concern and impatience.

"Your father, Tamara," she said. "What about your father? Tell me!"

It worked. Tami began shakily.

"He's acting stranger and stranger lately," she said. "I don't know what to do, or what he will do. He was always strict with me, but now . . ."

"He is not strict, Tami," Miriam interrupted her. "He is cruel!"

"No, no! You're wrong, Miriam," Tami protested. "You don't know my father. He is not cruel, not deep down. I know he loves me. He's just strange."

Miriam gripped her hand harder. He was strange all right.

"But since those last two times, when he caught me in your *shul*," Tami continued, "and when you came to my house looking for me, he is acting so weird. I'm afraid."

"What do you mean by weird?" Miriam asked.

"I'm never allowed out now, almost never. I can only go to school. I can't even visit the library, or you, or play, or anything. I'm becoming like a crazy person. Alone, alone all the time. Miriam, am I crazy?"

Miriam shook her head vigorously.

"No, Tami," she said. "You are not crazy at all."

Tamara, encouraged, burst forward.

"He goes for hours without talking, but I see him mum-bling to himself. He shuts the lights in the house and peers from behind the curtains, as though expecting someone to attack us. He hasn't even gone to work for the last two weeks."

"Then how did you get out now?"

"He had to go to a family wedding. I know he didn't want to go, but he had to. It was the cousin who brought him here after the war and helped us buy our house. He will be there until four or five o'clock. I was afraid, but it was my only chance to see you. Miriam, what should I do? I don't know what to do."

A car passed down the road, and both girls hid their faces like criminals. Tamara's fear had seeped into Miriam, but she tried not to show it.

"Tamara, I'll help you, I promise," she said. "We're in this together. We are pals, right? But you must help me also. There is big, big trouble in my house, too."

Tamara looked at Miriam curiously. Why was she so surprised, Miriam wondered, to hear that someone else has problems?

"Trouble?" asked Tami. "What trouble?"

"I know why your father is acting so strangely," said Miriam.

"You do?"

Another car roared down the road. The street was getting too busy. Miriam led Tamara back into one of the side roads. They stood along the edge of a steep river embankment, alone with the woods. Miriam decided to be direct.

"Your father did a terrible thing to my father," she said. "It was right after I visited you that *Shabbos*. He threatened to get even, and he did. He took my father's precious Torah. It's worth a fortune, and he knew how much it meant to us."

Tamara pulled back from Miriam, almost slipping into the river. Miriam caught her. She was angry.

"Miriam, my father wouldn't take something of yours," cried Tami. "He wouldn't take your Torah!"

"But he did!" answered Miriam angrily. "He did! I promise you. Who else threatened us? Who else would want it? Don't you see? He's all mixed up now, feeling guilty. That is why he has been acting strangely."

Tamara's face suddenly darkened with fright.

"If it's true, my father is in big trouble," she whispered. "Did you call the police?"

"No. My father didn't want to. He is afraid of the police. My parents don't know anything about your father. I never told them what happened when I visited your house that *Shabbos*. But if the Torah is not back soon, they'll have no choice. And then I'll have to tell them everything. Everything, you understand? Tamara, think! Do you know where your father hid it? Did he give any hint? Anything?"

Tamara paused and then came out with the strangest, calmest statement.

"Yes. I know exactly where it might be."

Miriam was shocked by Tamara's quiet certainty. But she did not press her, letting her explain at her own pace.

"Miriam, there is a room in the basement of our house. My father keeps it locked at all times. I am absolutely forbidden to go in. But once, I peered in when my father opened it. I was in the far corner of the cellar, and he didn't know I was there.

"There is absolutely nothing in the room but a large trunk. It's almost the size of a small closet but lying flat. That trunk is almost . . . almost . . . holy to my father. If he did take your Torah, he hid it there. I am sure of it."

Miriam despaired.

"But we will never be able to get in there if it is locked," she moaned.

"I know where the key is," said Tami. "I watched my

father once. We have two furnaces. One we use, the other is an old oil one. My father hid the key on top, in the dust. I know how to find it."

Miriam squeezed Tamara's hands so hard it must have hurt her.

"Then let's go there, Tami. Right now!"

Tamara recoiled with fright.

"No. I could never go."

"We must go, Tami, you and me. I am responsible for the Torah being taken."

Tamara was almost in tears.

"No, Miriam. I could never let you in the house myself. No one is allowed in our house."

"But your father is away. You said so yourself. He is away at a wedding. He won't be back until four or five o'clock. We have plenty of time. Tami, we must go now!"

"But, Miriam . . ."

"Tami, there's no time to lose. My father is getting sick over the missing Torah. He is not strong. Every hour counts. If they decide to call the police, your father will be arrested. He could go to jail . . ."

There was silence and a long pause. Both Miriam and Tamara were panting with nervousness. Then, barely moving, Tamara nodded her acceptance.

17 The Trunk in the Basement

TAMARA LOOKED EACH WAY TWICE TO MAKE SURE NO ONE was watching as she unlocked her front door. She slipped in with Miriam, as though they were breaking into a bank.

Tamara's house was very dark, like dusk. There was hardly a drop of color anywhere, just very pale walls and carpets of gray and brown. All the curtains were drawn, the windows shut tight. The air was stale and heavy. You could never tell what a gorgeous summer day was outside.

The only sound was the tick, tick, tick of an old grandfather clock.

"Follow me," whispered Tamara.

She led Miriam to the steps leading down to the cellar. A bare, dim light bulb dangled above the stairs. They clambered carefully down the narrow stairs to the basement. It was gray and dusty, and the cinder blocks of the foundation lay bare. The front window was totally blocked with a wooden board. Two dull light bulbs provided all the lighting.

There was an old furnace in the back of the room, covered with a layer of dust. Alongside were some boards and cans. Behind them was a bare wall, with a white wooden door in the middle.

"That's the room," Tamara said.

"We have to get in," Miriam insisted.

Tamara stared at the door as though it were a holy object. Miriam could feel her fear. She waited. Tamara must feel like she's entering the *Kodesh Kadashim*, she thought.

"I . . . I've never gone in there before. If my father catches me, he'll kill me."

"But your father is not here," Miriam pressed her. "You are saving him from much worse trouble, from the police!"

Tamara led Miriam to the old furnace. It looked cold and dead. Covering the top was a white layer of dust. Tamara moved a pail next to the furnace, carefully stood on it and groped her fingers over the top of the furnace. She climbed back down, her hands covered with dust. She had two keys.

"One is for the door," Tamara explained. "I think the other is for the trunk."

"Let's hurry," Miriam urged, her heart racing. If she could discover her father's Torah, she would be ecstatic.

Tamara's hands were slippery with dust, and she fumbled with the key. Finally, it slipped in and turned, and she carefully opened the door.

The room was the size of a small bedroom. The same switch that turned on the lights outside also lit a small bulb in the room. It was absolutely empty, no furniture, no boards or cans. Just one object lay in the middle of the floor, a large trunk.

There was something odd about the room. What was it? Something different. Miriam's eyes widened with wonder and curiosity. Then she knew.

The room was spotless, perfect. Someone has brushed away every spot, every drop of dust, like a *shul* before *Yom Kippur*.

Tamara was almost trembling as they approached the trunk. Miriam took her hand. She knew how hard and scary this was for her. She took the second key and inserted it into the trunk lock.

"Hurry, hurry," whispered Miriam. She had absorbed Tamara's fear and was very frightened now. "Hurry!"

"What are you doing here?"

Miriam and Tamara spun around. Standing in the doorway, his thin face screwed in fury, was Tamara's father.

"What are you two doing here?" he repeated. His voice roared, and he looked like a madman.

"Daddy!" cried Tamara with fright. "I didn't mean to do it. I was just showing Miriam—"

"You little devil," he hissed at Miriam. "What are you doing in my house without permission?"

He drew closer, blocking any escape. Shaking, Miriam stepped back, frozen in paralyzing fear.

"What are you doing here?" he demanded, again and again. "What are you doing in my house, in this room?"

He drew closer and Miriam tried to scream, but it choked in her throat. Her mouth flew open, but nothing came out.

Kranz glared like a tiger into her eyes.

"Don't lay a finger on her!"

Rabbi Levi stood at the entrance to the little room. His great frame, his long black coat and great white beard seemed to fill the whole doorway. Miriam broke away from Kranz and ran to her father's side. Kranz was first stunned, then he roared like a wounded animal. He rushed at Miriam's father, his fist raised.

Just as he was about to strike, Rabbi Levi swung his great hand and slapped Kranz across the face. It was such a hard impact that the crack echoed for a second in the room.

His face already turning purple from the blow, Kranz tottered back and stared in confusion. Then he lifted his hand to his face and began weeping like a child.

"Daddy!" cried Tamara.

She ran to her father's side and took his hand to comfort him. Each girl stood at her father's side like the coaches of two prizefighters.

Rabbi Levi calmed Miriam, walked over to Mr. Kranz and gently placed his great hands on Kranz's thin shoulders.

"I am ashamed that I struck you," he said. "Come, let us sit down together."

He led him to the closed trunk, the only seat in the room.

"No, not there," Kranz protested weakly, almost in a whisper.

He was still weeping and seemed dazed. Rabbi Levi forced him to sit down.

"Tamara," Rabbi Levi ordered. "Please get a wet washcloth and a glass of water for your father."

In seconds, Tamara was back. Mr. Kranz began regaining control of himself. He wiped his face but waved away the glass of water. He turned to Miriam's father.

"I am also sorry I tried to strike you," he said. "It was a great disrespect to a rabbi. But what are you doing in my house?"

"I saw my daughter enter your home a few minutes ago to play with your daughter," said Rabbi Levi. "When I saw you come home a few minutes later, I was afraid there might be a misunderstanding, after all the trouble we've had. So I knocked on your door, but there was no answer. Only when I heard the yelling coming from the basement window did I run downstairs."

Miriam was stunned. So her father had been watching her all the time. And she thought she had been so clever.

The old anger seeped into Mr. Kranz's voice, like Shimshon regaining his power.

"You say the girls came here to play?" he roared. "Look around you. Is this a playroom? Are there games here? If they came to play, they had a whole house. No, they had trouble in mind, bad mischief. Why else are they down here now?"

There was silence, and Rabbi Levi looked at Miriam. His eyes demanded an answer.

Miriam hesitated, not sure how much to reveal. Tamara stared at her, alarm in her eyes. Mr. Kranz sat bowed and shrunken and angry. Rabbi Levi burned with impatience. There was no way out. Miriam turned to Tamara's father.

"You know what we came here for, Mr. Kranz," she said. "We want our *Sefer Torah* back."

He gaped at her, puzzled.

"Your Torah? What Torah?"

Miriam finally lost her temper. All the worry and danger she had felt for weeks and months spilled out of her.

"You know, Mr. Kranz! The Torah you stole from my father's *shul*! The one you have hidden right under you, in this trunk. That is the Torah I want!"

Rabbi Levi's eyes widened and his face reddened. He ran over to Kranz and loomed large and fearsome over him.

"You took the Torah? It was you, then?"

Mr. Kranz stood up angrily.

"What are you all talking about?" he asked. "What Torah?"

"A precious scroll was taken from our synagogue," Rabbi Levi explained. "There was no one else angry at us except you."

Mr. Kranz's fighting spirit revived fully. His face grew stern and sly.

"I swear you're all crazy," he said. "Take your Torah? What business do I have with your Torah? Who wants your Torah? Is that why you broke into my house? Is that why?"

He turned to Miriam, glaring.

"Haven't you made enough trouble?" he seethed. "Is that why you violated this private room? Is that why, you meddler?"

From somewhere, Miriam summoned up great *chutzpah*.

"I don't believe you, Mr. Kranz!" she blurted.

"My father doesn't lie," Tamara suddenly hissed.

Miriam stared at her. She couldn't believe her ears. He was so mean to her, yet Tamara was defending her father. Rabbi Levi tried to calm the situation. There was uncertainty in his voice.

"If it is true that you do not have the Torah," he said, "would you mind opening the trunk and letting us see what is in there? Just to remove any doubt?"

"Very well, but I will show it only to you." He turned to Tamara. "You and this little girl go upstairs. Leave us alone."

There was a pause. Tamara met her father, eye to eye.

"No, Daddy," she said.

He glowered at her and raised his voice threateningly.

"Get out! Go upstairs!"

"No, Daddy. No more. I can't any more. I can't."

She moved from her father's side and huddled near Miriam.

Kranz gave her a long, stern look. Her eyes locked into his, almost maniacally. They showed no fear. Something had burst in Tamara. A shell had cracked, and a new Tamara emerged, very strong, very sure. He shrugged, angry but defeated.

He took the key from Tamara, thrust it into the lock and turned it open. He opened the lid and unceremoniously dumped a pile of old clothing on the floor. Lying on the bottom of the trunk was a small bundle, carefully wrapped in white paper, bound by a single cord. Kranz gently lifted the bundle, undid the cord and unfolded the paper, revealing a blue child's dress. Its color had faded, and it gave off a musty smell. It was made of linen and had white lace on the hem and sleeves, now faded gray.

Tamara approached her father and carefully touched the dress.

"Whose dress was that?" she asked.

He smiled at her, very, very sadly.

"This dress belonged to your Aunt Tamara."

Tamara's eyes widened.

"Aunt Tamara? I didn't know I had an Aunt Tamara."

The strange, faraway look, the sad smile did not leave her father's face.

"Long before you were born, years ago, in Poland. She was my younger sister. When I was eleven, she was just nine. She even looked like you."

"What happened to her?" pressed Tamara.

"She was so beautiful. She had two lovely braids and a pearl butterfly that she wore on the side of her hair. She sang the most beautiful *Shabbos* songs and was much better in school than I was. She could even read the *Chumash*. She was so sweet, never harmed the smallest fly."

"What happened?" asked Rabbi Levi solemnly.

Mr. Kranz snorted with anger. His gaze went far beyond the cellar room, to a different time and place.

"Was she taken away in a Nazi transport?" Miriam's father breathed gently.

"Taken away?" He stared at him as though the rabbi were a child. "Taken away? They took her and my three little cousins Chavie, Esther and Moishe. They stood them against a wall and used them for target practice. I ran away and hid before they could catch me. But I saw everything. I heard her scream and fall. I . . . I heard the screams . . ."

A deep silence fell in the room.

"This one dress I took from our house later that night. It was the only thing I had to remember her by. I stuffed it into my bag and ran off with some older boys into the forest. I kept this dress all these years. It is all I have left from my whole family. A whole family in one poor, little dress."

His head dropped, and he held the dress tightly to himself. Tamara ran to be at her father's side. Rabbi Levi said nothing at first. Finally, he turned to Kranz. There was great respect in his voice.

"One thing I do not understand in all this," he said. "The Almighty blessed you with a beautiful child. She is a wonderful young girl and even bears your sister's holy name. Why have you been so harsh with your daughter? Why have you made her life so miserable?"

"Harsh? I have not been harsh to her," answered Kranz

curtly. "Ever since her mother passed away when she was just a little baby, I have raised her all by myself, and I have done her a great kindness, a great favor."

"Favor? What favor?"

"I have taught her about real life. I have taught her what to expect from life. I am making her strong. I have not been soft with her, because when she goes into the real world, she will see that there are wild animals ready to pounce and hurt and destroy. I have given her a taste of the real world, not a dream world that will leave her helpless later on."

"But you have become your daughter's worst enemy," argued Rabbi Levi. "You have not been a father, but a jailer."

"I have been her teacher!" Kranz shot back. "If our parents had prepared us to be tougher, then we would have been better prepared to meet our enemies."

Kranz turned his gaze from Rabbi Levi to Tamara. There was very deep sadness on his face.

"Am I your enemy, Tamara?" he asked pathetically. "Is that what you think of me?"

She held his hand tightly.

"Daddy, I love you," she said simply.

Rabbi Levi approached Kranz and placed his large hands on the small, faded dress.

"My friend, this is the past, sad and old," he said. "Your little girl is the future, bright and lovely. If you really want her to be strong, let her fulfill the yearning in her heart for the sweet taste of the Torah. Let her be my Miriam's friend. Let her come to us."

Kranz's eyes were downcast. He look tired and pale. His eyes went from the dress to Tamara, back and forth, back and forth. His chest heaved as though something inside him were bursting to come out. He nodded.

"*Baruch Hashem*," sighed Rabbi Levi.

As Miriam and her father shuffled out of the house together he whispered softly to her.

"We have learned a great lesson today, you and I. We misjudged Mr. Kranz, thinking he was just a cruel man."

"But he was so mean, Tati! I'm glad you hit him."

"No, Miriam," said Rabbi Levi. "We forget that even people who seem as senseless as Mr. Kranz have a story, a past that makes them act that way."

"Well, he certainly looked like he was just being mean."

"That's true. But we're Torah Jews, and we should have been kinder and looked beyond appearances. I have a feeling that Mr. Kranz has a very deep *neshamah*, but I must get to know him better. You'll see, Miriam, it will yet be good. Yes, I hope it will be very good."

18 The Atom Bomb Satchel

A HUGE CLOUD HAD LIFTED FROM THE LEVI FAMILY. EVEN with the Torah still missing, Miriam's father was in an elevated, joyous mood. A Torah was missing, but a Jewish child had been found; Kranz had given permission for Tamara to begin Hebrew lessons with Miriam. Rabbi Levi hummed contentedly to himself as he studied.

But Leah Levi was not at peace. The next day, she confided to Miriam the reason for her sudden uneasiness.

"I suspected all along that Mr. Kranz had taken the Torah as an act of revenge," she said. "As long as it was in his hands, I knew it would come to no harm. But now, who knows where the Torah is?"

"How could you be sure Mr. Kranz wouldn't damage it?" pressed Miriam.

"It was just how I felt about him," said Mrs. Levi. "I thought it possible that he might try to hurt us, but he would be afraid to lift a hand against the Torah. I told your father, and we watched you very closely. You did not notice. When you received the note from Tamara, we felt we were on the right track. We hoped it might lead to the Torah."

"So did I," Miriam answered. She laughed. "We all had our secrets. But why doesn't Tati call the police?"

Her mother sighed.

"You're right," she said. "But your father is afraid of the police."

Miriam's mother now showed a side of her that Miriam had not seen before. Leah always showed great respect for her husband, almost like to a father. After all, he was more than ten years older than her. But now, she did not give him any peace. She started before breakfast, continued through lunch, persisted past supper and even interrupted him late at night as he pored over the pages of the Talmud.

"Mordechai, we dare not wait any longer," she insisted. "The trail will grow ice cold if we continue to delay. We must call the police immediately."

"We shall see," he answered noncommittally.

"There is no time to see," she responded stubbornly. "The time to see and wait has passed. Someone has our precious Torah. We must call the police now, not tomorrow, not in the morning. The police can be here in a few minutes; they can begin a search."

"No," he answered firmly. "Who knows what it will lead to? What questions? What investigations?"

So it went, the whole day, the whole night. Miriam was not in the habit of eavesdropping on her parents' conversations, but she couldn't help overhearing them. She pitied her father. Her mother was right, of course. But it was hard for her Tati. That was the way he was, gentle, kind, a man of books, of a quiet word. He was so afraid of police and reports and investigations. The murmuring of their arguments grew louder and louder. Her parents had never raised their voices at each other, but now they were almost shouting.

Tuesday morning broke, and Miriam went down to the kitchen. It was past nine o'clock, and her father had already returned from *Shacharis*. He looked haggard.

"What happened?" Miriam asked.

Her mother gave a triumphant but discreet look.

"Tati agreed to call the police right after breakfast."

Miriam looked at her father, who was *bentching*. He looked very nervous and uncomfortable. As soon as he finished, he wiped his mouth with a napkin and rose with determination.

"If it must be done, it must be done," he muttered.

He went into the den, closed the door and spoke on the phone for a few minutes. The door opened, and he stood grim-faced.

"They said they will send someone as soon as they can," he reported. "Since there is no emergency, it may take a while. There is nothing to do but wait. Miriam, please bring me my *sefer*."

Miriam ran down to the *shul* and brought up a thick, old *sefer* bound in a black cover with gold lettering.

Rabbi Levi sat at the breakfast table, turned his back to his troubles and lost himself in his studies.

But just for a few moments. Outside, a horn blew persistently. Rabbi Levi closed the *sefer* with a sigh. The world had intruded again.

"It must be the police," he said as he stood up.

"Strange," remarked Leah. "You would think they'd have the courtesy to ring the bell."

The whole family marched to the front hallway and opened the door.

"Oh, no," groaned Leah, holding her head.

Even Rabbi Levi's face fell. Outside was not the police but a running taxi. It was Luzer, back from his Montreal trip. He and the taxi driver were struggling to extricate the atom bomb satchel from the trunk. Luzer turned and waved merrily.

"I just arrived in Toronto a half-hour ago, downtown at the bus station," he called out. "I haven't eaten anything yet. Maybe I can have some breakfast? I have nothing prepared at home."

Leah Levi lost her patience.

"Mordechai, I can't have him now," she said. "The police will be here in a few minutes. Everything that happens here will be all over town. We'll never get rid of him. Please!"

"Please, Tati," Miriam chimed in. "Not Luzer, not now."

Rabbi Levi kept his voice down.

"But the poor man must be famished," he said. "It's a six-hour ride from Montreal. Where could he find kosher food on the way? Let's at least give him a bagel and a piece of herring. He will most likely be gone before the police come."

The argument didn't matter anyway. Luzer had paid the taxi driver and, still beaming, dragged the monstrous bag halfway towards the front steps. There was no way to refuse.

"Come in, Luzer," Leah said, hiding her chagrin. "We're quite busy, but we'll find something."

It was becoming warm, and Luzer perspired like a fountain as he carried the satchel up the steps. With a sigh of relief, he set it down on the hallway floor, blocking the entrance. Rabbi Levi came over with a cold glass of orange juice. Miriam squeezed around the bag and peered towards Bathurst Street, watching for the police.

Luzer took off his floppy, wide-brimmed hat, wiped the perspiration from beneath his enormous greasy black velvet *yarmulka*, made a *berachah* and gulped down the juice.

"Oy, I needed that," he said with a sigh.

"Come, Luzer," Leah called impatiently from the kitchen. "I set something up for you. Come quickly, please. We are in a big rush this morning."

"Oh, thank you," said Luzer eagerly, rubbing his hands with excitement.

He rushed to the kitchen sink and lifted the washing cup. He smiled at the family.

"I'll show you the cover later," he added.

He filled the cup and began washing his hands. He didn't notice three people staring at him in puzzlement.

"What cover?" asked Leah.

But it was too late. Luzer had washed his hands already and couldn't speak out until he got to his bagel. He raised his index finger to gesture that "in a moment I'll tell you everything."

Rabbi Levi quickly handed him a bagel.

"What cover, Luzer?" he demanded. "Say *Hamotzi*, quick!"

Luzer dipped the bagel three times in the air, signalling that he needed salt. Miriam brought him a salt shaker, and he carefully poured a few sprinkles on the table and dipped in his bagel.

"What cover, Luzer?" Leah pressed.

But Luzer wasn't finished. He couldn't talk because his mouth was stuffed with bagel. The family watched each biting motion of his chubby cheeks as he struggled to swallow the piece of bagel. Finally, he swallowed, gulped and grinned.

"Didn't Dizzy tell you?"

"Tell us what?" Rabbi Levi asked, trying to stay calm.

"Oy, wonderful!" Luzer beamed. "Then it will be a surprise."

"What surprise?" begged Leah, almost in tears. "Tell us the surprise, please!"

"Come," Luzer said triumphantly.

He led the family to the atom bomb satchel in the hallway, fussed with the rusty clasps and snapped it open. As he undid the parcel, he muttered half to himself and half to the family.

"I told Dizzy before we left that I was going to borrow the Torah for a few days," said Luzer. "He said it was fine."

Rabbi Levi grew pale.

"Dizzy said it was fine to borrow the Torah? Dizzy?"

"Yes. He promised to tell you, but he must have forgotten. What a *tzazkeleh*! So forgetful. Here . . ."

He lifted out a package wrapped in brown paper, the size of the Torah. He cradled it in his arms like a baby.

"Come," he announced. "I'll open it downstairs, in the *shul*."

Miriam looked up at her parents. Their eyes were moist. Miriam, too, was crying quietly, thanking Hashem. They filed downstairs. Luzer placed the package gently on the table, took out a penknife and carefully cut the cord that held the wrapping in place. He began uncovering layer after layer of brown paper. As he removed the paper, he explained.

"Do you remember the *Shabbos* you named that little girl Devorah?" He pulled off yet more paper. "You spoke about how every Jew must care for the next person. Those were holy words. Anyway, I have a cousin in Montreal. She's a wonderful artist. Here . . ."

Luzer exposed the Torah.

Rabbi Levi held his breath. In place of the old, shabby mantel was a beautiful deep purple cover, inscribed with glistening gold letters: *"Ve'ahavta lerayacha kamocha,"* you shall love your neighbor as yourself. On the bottom, in small Hebrew letters, was the dedication: "Donated by Eluzer ben Yaakov in honor of the Levi Family who live these words."

"It's incredible," Leah gasped. "Mordechai, I never saw anything so beautiful in my life!"

"It is the only one of its kind in the world," Luzer announced proudly. "My cousin Malka made it special."

Rabbi Levi stared and stared at it, speechless and moist-eyed. Even Luzer appeared shaken by the enormity of what he had done and how he had touched his rabbi.

"Do you think Luzer only takes and never gives?" he asked.

Rabbi Levi did not, could not, answer. He squeezed Luzer's shoulders with gratitude. He took a deep breath, and then his face opened into a deep smile, a smile that flooded his lips, his mouth, his eyes, his great forehead and brows, his whole being.

Upstairs, the doorbell rang.

"It's the police," Leah murmured. "They finally came."

"Tati, I'll go up to them," Miriam offered.

Rabbi Levi looked down at Miriam and smiled.

"No, I will go up to meet them myself," he said. "I want to tell them that nothing is wrong. In fact, everything is very good!"